"Was a pleasure reading [this] book. As one who is very interested in the Civil War...I find the times and some of the language right on. The book takes you on a journey as if you were looking down from heaven watching the story unfold. It would make an exciting movie."

—Elliott Barnett, Corpsman, U. S. Navy (Ret.)

"As a lover of historical novels, I was fortunate...to preview *KILL THE DEVIL*. The story [is] woven with just the right amount of twists and turns...to keep me eagerly turning the pages. It was a thoroughly enjoyable read that I would recommend to all readers of good fiction."

—Ron Seaman, (PA) Township Manager

KILL THE DEVIL

KILL THE DEVIL

T. K. MARION

A Novel of the War Between the States

ISBN 978-0-6151-4793-2
Thirteen Stars Press
Printed in the United States of America

Marketing-PR Consultant Trish Doll, Publicity Works
Book cover and logo by Deb Deysher, Double D Media
Photograph by Steve Garber (a.k.a. Steve G)

You are invited to visit the author's web site at
www.tkmarion.com

In memory of my father, whose legacy as a loving husband, devoted father and career naval officer will be forever deserving of Almighty God.

He is my hero.

AUTHOR'S NOTE

The Civil War was the most consequential episode in American history. The four years of bloodshed, brought about by political dissent between North and South on the issue of slavery, claimed the lives of more that 600,000 soldiers. When the shooting ended, Abraham Lincoln's goal to reunite the nation was realized. Eight months following the great emancipator's death, the institution of slavery was officially stricken from the American conscience with the passing of the Thirteenth Amendment to the Constitution.

This book is a work of fiction. The inclusion of real players of the period such as Lincoln, Ulysses S. Grant and Robert E. Lee was essential to complement the story line and offer the reader an imagery of realism. An attempt to revise history or impress upon one that the events in this book are factual was never the intent of this writer.

"As commander in chief in time of war, I suppose I have a right to take any measure which may subdue the enemy."

Abraham Lincoln

I

The President of the United States of America had a terrible headache.

It had started the night before while he and members of his war cabinet were locked in heated debate. The topic of discussion was the result of the latest action dispatches from northern Virginia, where fierce fighting had erupted near Cedar Creek two days previous. Included in the reports was an estimate of the number of casualties associated with the bloody battle. All of the fallen were Americans—the cream of the nation.

Abraham Lincoln closed his eyes and gently massaged the tender area at the side of his head. Yes, the war had dragged on much too long. Tragically, it would be his legacy, his chapter in the history books long after he was dead and buried. Had he been wrong in allowing it to continue so long? Four generations of brave men were fighting and dying for him every minute of every day, and he had to put a stop to it. Only how? What was the answer?

"We must continue to starve the South into submission," one of his senior cabinet officials had suggested. "When that happens, Jeff Davis will have no recourse but to accept our surrender terms," added the Secretary of War.

Abe shook his head. No, Mr. Stanton's idea hadn't worked, isn't working and wouldn't work in the future. Crafty old Bobby Lee would somehow find a way to feed his troops, even if they had to eat the dirt out of the ground. What he needed was a faster solution, a quick military solution that would end the senseless slaughter once and for all. Perhaps the man due at the White House this morning would have the answer.

God, I hope so!

Ulysses Simpson Grant arrived at the White House ten minutes later than expected. He looked tired, even more so than the last time Lincoln had seen him. He seemed thinner too, as if he hadn't consumed a nourishing meal since last week. Abe smirked, noting the bloodshot eyes of the man with the unkempt dark beard. Had the general been drinking his favorite brand of whiskey again?

"You're looking well, Mr. President," said the top soldier of the Union army. He showed the cigar in his hand. "Mind if I smoke?"

Lincoln nodded indifferently and gave his attention to the man who had accompanied Grant to the meeting. Joshua Stairs was the general's aide-de-camp, a much younger man than both he and Grant. His chestnut brown hair showed no evidence of premature gray, and the blue uniform he wore seemed a perfect fit, unlike the general's which hung from his person like a wilted flower. Abe saw purpose in the soldier's green eyes as he stepped closer and held out his hand.

"A pleasure to see you again, Major."

"An honor, Mr. President."

Lincoln indicated the chair by the window, next to Grant. "Please sit down, won't you?"

"I'm perfectly fine, sir."

"As you wish." Abe cleared the gravel from his throat. "Shall we get down to business, gentlemen?"

Grant said, "Mr. President, I met with my staff last night to discuss our chances of winning the war before Christmas. The consensus was that it's militarily impossible."

"The Confederacy is starving, General. We've five times the resources, we outnumber them two to one in the field, and have far better weaponry. What is it that keeps them together and fighting? I must know the answer."

"Sir, you already know the answer." Grant lit the cigar. "The real question is what are we going to do about him?"

"He must be destroyed," said Stairs, joining in. "Robert E. Lee *must* be destroyed. If we eliminate him, the South will collapse."

"Killing one soldier would end the war?" Abe grunted. "No, I can't believe that."

"Sir, General Lee is no ordinary soldier. He represents the heart and soul of the Confederate army. His troops regard him as a saint, a godlike figure. Before the war he was America's top soldier."

"And perhaps still is," added Grant with a smirk. "Wish I had such loyalty from my troops."

"Your service to the cause has been invaluable," Lincoln told him. "Perhaps if I'd chosen you to lead the army earlier, the war would be over by now."

"Those are kind words, Mr. President," Grant said to the cigar. "However, getting back to the business at hand, I truly believe the major's suggestion is worthy of serious consideration. If we eliminate Lee, the South would knuckle under and give up the fight. Let's face it, who would lead them on the battlefield?"

"Are you suggesting that we assassinate Lee?"

It was Stairs who answered, "If you want to end the war and save lives, it's the best solution."

Lincoln frowned at him, thinking how indifferent he seemed. A harsh product of the war? He rubbed his temple with more vigor.

"But how can we be sure that killing Lee is the answer? Besides, the word assassination leaves a bad taste on my palate."

"Lee is the enemy, sir. If he dies, he dies like any soldier serving his country. Does it really matter how?"

Grant said, "Mr. President, if Lee is killed, the South may continue the struggle for a while, but without his leadership the Reb army would eventually crumble and surrender.

Thousands on both sides would be spared. Then we can start the process of rebuilding the country. Isn't that what the war is all about?"

"Yes, General, you're absolutely right." Lincoln clapped him on the shoulder. "Now why don't you get something to eat? Looks to me like you could stand a hearty meal. We'll speak of this business again tomorrow." A fleeting smile. "Thank you both for coming."

Later that evening as he sat in the rocking chair by the fireplace, the president was pensive. Would he have enough backbone to order the assassination of General Lee? Would the man's death bring about the downfall of the Confederacy and begin the nation's healing process? Was it his only option?

He sighed. God, he felt tired—and older. It was almost as if the brain had stopped working altogether. No, he did not have a viable solution to end the war, but he had to find one; it was his duty. The daily bloodshed at the front lines had to be stopped. And if killing Lee was the answer...

His wife appeared in the sitting room, a red shawl tucked under her right arm. She wore a pretty velvet and white dress befitting of her expensive taste in fashion, her dark hair arranged in a taut bun. Mary Todd Lincoln seemed in a gay mood, her oval face attached to a broad smile.

"Evening, dear," she said. "Feeling better?"

"Not much," he said to the folded hands on his lap.

"Perhaps it's time you went to bed. Tomorrow will be a better day, surely."

She kissed him on the cheek, and he smiled in return. She draped the shawl over his shoulders, kissed him again, and he watched as she strolled out of the room, wondering how she could be so calm.

You just don't understand, my dear.

The president shut his eyes and rocked in the chair.

Ulysses S. Grant poured himself a small brandy. He stared at the tumbler for a moment, as if undecided what to do with it. At last he lifted the glass to his lips and drank. He put the empty tumbler down and faced his aide-de-camp, who was standing at the opposite side of the map table.

"Well, Major, I know you're dying to tell me what you're thinking, so get on with it."

"Sir, the president will not give the order to assassinate Lee unless you apply the necessary pressure," said Joshua Stairs. "He respects your opinion more than any other soldier in the army."

Grant dismissed the compliment with a grunt and lit a cigar.

Stairs heard him say, "Have you worked out the details of your plan with my staff in case the president decides to go through with it?"

"No, General, you told me to keep the idea to myself. The fewer who know about it, the better. Were not those your exact words?"

"But you do have an action plan prepared?"

"Yes, sir, I do. The plan would require a small team of handpicked men. About a half dozen, I think. All would be expert sharpshooters, elite cavalrymen."

"A hit-and-run raid?"

"Yes, sir."

"But what you're suggesting sounds like a suicide mission. I'm not so sure I could muster up the courage to order six men to risk their lives for something that may prove fruitless in the end."

"You wouldn't need to, sir. Those assigned would be volunteers to a man."

"But who would volunteer for a job like this knowing they might never return?"

"Patriots, General, men dedicated to the noble cause of victory."

"Indeed!" Grant allowed himself a moment of thought. "And a man to lead this daring raid?"

"I've several in mind, but one in particular."

"Go on."

"His name is Westmoreland—Captain Jonathan Westmoreland. If you recall, sir, he was a member of your staff during the latter stage of the Vicksburg campaign. At the moment he's serving in the Thirteenth Pennsylvania Regiment. A veteran horse soldier and rifleman."

"And holder of the Congressional Medal of Honor."

"Yes, sir. I'll never forget that day his cavalry charge routed the enemy flank at Shiloh. It was a thing of military genius. How many lives were saved, not to mention the number of prisoners that were taken? For my money, Jon Westmoreland is the perfect man for the job."

"Where is he now?"

"Well, sir, there's a small problem. He's presently on furlough. I was told that it's his first leave since we took Vicksburg last year."

"When is he due back with his regiment?"

"In three days."

"Very well. Have him sent for as soon as he returns."

"I've already done that, General. I thought you'd agree with my choice, so I've arranged to meet with him on the day he gets back."

"You're as thorough as ever, Major."

Smiling, Grant fixed a brandy for his aide and gave it to him. Stairs thanked him, raised the tumbler to his mouth and drank.

At that moment Jonathan Westmoreland was enjoying life. The day before he had adopted the institution of marriage into his life. His bride, barely twenty years old, was the cousin of his sister's best friend and daughter of a protestant Welsh minister. Westmoreland had turned twenty-four just three months earlier. A young man, and yet a veteran soldier of three years in the field.

The wedding had been a private affair, a small ceremony in the church of his grandparents with mostly relatives attending. The only person missing was his brother, Peter, who had died of shrapnel wounds at Gettysburg two summers previous. His only brother, Peter was to have been his best man.

He stared at his sleeping bride. Her lovely face showed a portrait of contentment, telling him that there was nothing more she required out of life. He smiled as he recalled the day they met. It was over a year ago, two months before the bloodbath at Gettysburg happened.

The church picnic was crowded, with dozens of pretty women ripe for the picking, but it was Alice Medwin who had caught his particular attention. She was so beautiful in her blue spring dress, her long, flowing hair the color of wet oak. She was so polite and formal at first, but when they walked hand in hand later by the brook she poured out her heart to him: of her desire for a happy life and to bear children someday for the man she would marry. Now, incredibly, seventeen months had passed since that wonderful afternoon, during which he had lost a brother but gained a loving wife. But that was life, an amazing process of ups and downs, good and bad. Like the war.

She stirred beside him and came awake, her silky hair sliding across his bare shoulder as she lifted her head. He could see the sparkle in her eyes but not their blue color. She was a simple girl, and yet intelligent and mature, far beyond her years. Perhaps that's why he loved her, why he needed her so much. She was the missing piece in his life ever since Peter had gone…

"Mmm!" she purred. "You're awake, darling."

"Was just watching you," he said. "Go back to sleep."

She ran her fingers over his chin, barely making contact, and he heard her say, "I love you, Jonathan. What were you thinking of? Tell me, I need to know. I'm your wife now, I need to know everything."

"We'll talk about it in the morning."

Alice Westmoreland brought her naked body closer, her

firm breasts pressing against him, and caressed his earlobe with her wandering lips.

"Please tell me," she said. "I won't be able to sleep unless you do."

"Was just thinking how lucky I am to have you as my wife."

"I had a wonderful dream, Jonathan. I dreamt that we had been blessed with our first child. It was a boy—our son." She smiled hugely. "Do you like that dream?"

"Of course," he said, smiling back. "Tell me, did you have a name for our son in your dream?"

"That I don't remember. All I remember is that the war was over and we had our first child. He was beautiful, darling. He had your gray eyes and dark hair, your character and strength of will."

"And your beautiful smile, no doubt." He planted a kiss on her forehead. "Was our son as smart as her mother?"

"Smarter. Someday he'll be an important man, just like his father. Perhaps a doctor or a teacher...or maybe a soldier."

"I'm not that important," he said glumly. "I don't like being a soldier anymore."

"After the war you'll be important, darling, especially to our children and me. You'll be an important engineer and build many railroads and bridges. They will bring people closer together and make the country grow and be strong. And that's important, *very* important."

"When the war's over, there will be much rebuilding to do, particularly in the south."

"I thank God every day that I don't live in the south. It

must be awful for all the people there."

"Yes, we're both lucky, Alice. Southern people are starving because of the river blockades. I saw the worst of it in Mississippi when I served at Vicksburg with General Grant. And it's not much better in Virginia, yet the war goes on somehow."

"I sometimes wonder why God allows it to continue," she said, speaking to the ceiling. "It just doesn't seem right."

"I know what you mean."

He smiled as she pillowed her head on his chest, enjoying the nakedness of her. Yes, she was a simple girl, bright, mature, far beyond her years. She saw what he saw, wanted what he wanted. His smile grew with pride as he pictured her as the mother of his children. No doubt she would be the perfect mother. She would love and nurture them with solid Christian values, and nothing less. That in itself was comforting.

She was asleep, he could tell. He kissed her again, thinking of their future and how happy he was to be alive. Then he thought of Peter and the countless other American brothers who had lost their lives in combat—on both sides.

Dear God, how much longer?

II

braham Lincoln arranged another meeting in the White House the following morning. In attendance were "Sam" Grant, Joshua Stairs and the Secretary of War. The topic of discussion was the same as the day previous.

"Eliminating Lee will accomplish two things," said Lincoln's cabinet secretary. "First of all, the South will be without a leader to direct its army. By the time Jeff Davis finds a suitable replacement, we will have taken command of the field."

"Agreed," said Stairs. "Without Lee the Reb army will dissolve."

Lincoln seemed not to have heard him.

"And the second thing it will accomplish?" he asked the Secretary of War.

"The matter of enemy morale," replied Edwin Stanton. "When word of Lee's death is announced, it will spread through the south like a plague. Their armies would be in disarray, not to mention the effect it would have on the citizenry."

"But what if Lee's death produces the opposite effect?" challenged the president. "Mr. Davis just might use Lee as a martyr to inspire his troops."

"I think that highly unlikely," said Stanton. "They would still need someone to lead them in the field. And that man doesn't exist, at least not of Lee's caliber."

Lincoln turned to Grant. The hero of the battles of Vicksburg and Chattanooga had been conspicuously silent during the exchange. He just stood there calm as a statue, as if waiting for the right moment to voice his opinion. Abe wanted to hear it then.

"Well, General?"

"Mr. President, with all due respect to Secretary Stanton, the question of Confederate morale is pure conjecture. However, I do agree with him regarding the matter of command. The enemy has no one capable of filling Lee's shoes. Davis would have his hands full trying to find his successor."

Stairs said, "May I add something, Mr. President?"

"Please do, Major."

"Thank you." Stairs swallowed the lump in his throat. "Sir,

I'm a career soldier. I swore an oath to do my duty in wartime and in peace. As the general knows, I served at Vicksburg—a bloody campaign. I lost a brother and two cousins there, along with scores of good fighting men of my regiment. Many left wives and children behind. Each one gave the supreme sacrifice."

"I'm well aware of the consequences of this war," Lincoln told him. "I share the pain of the bereaved." An impatient sigh. "So what's your point?"

"Simply this. The general asked me to create a plan that would end the war as quickly as possible. In my opinion, destroying Lee is the only option available to us at this time. Each minute we debate the issue causes lives to be lost in the field."

Grant said, "Mr. President, no one has greater respect for General Lee than I. We served together in the Mexican War."

"I appreciate that, General."

Grant continued, "Major Stairs has done his duty. I believe his plan to eliminate Lee has a fair chance of success. If we do succeed, we'll be that much closer to winning the war."

Lincoln stroked his beard, knowing Grant was right. But the decision to go forward with Stairs' plan was his to make. He could never allow the general the burden of ordering the execution of a fellow officer and former comrade-in-arms, even though the man *was* serving on the opposite side of the battlefield. After all, Robert E. Lee was an American.

"Gentlemen, last week Mr. Horace Greeley, distinguished editor of the *New York Tribune*, wrote another letter to this office urging me to stop the war. Since then I've been asking myself just how I would go about it. Needless to say, I had no answer." The president confronted Grant. "General, I respect your judgment more than any other soldier in the army. You have my endorsement to evaluate this matter with more scrutiny and proceed at your discretion. Good luck."

Later that morning in the comfort of his private railway car, Grant met with Stairs to hash out the details of their new project. In front of them was a small rectangular table, a situation map of northern Virginia spread out on top. Stairs had the floor.

"General, in order for my plan to succeed, we must get started at once. There can be no further delay."

"Agreed," nodded Grant. "If we're successful, the war could be over by the end of the year."

"Yes, sir, a strong possibility."

"I've thought about the men who will take part in this assignment," said Grant, addressing the map. "In particular, their chances of getting back alive."

"You don't believe they will, do you, sir?"

"No. In fact, I'd be surprised if they're able to get close enough for one shot at Lee."

"But, General, we *must* try."

"And we will, Major. But I want those who volunteer for this job to be unmarried men. You agree?"

"I've decided to let Captain Westmoreland handle that."

"Very well." Grant lit a cigar. "Now let's review your plan one more time."

*　　*　　*

Jon Westmoreland awoke that morning to the scent of cooked bacon in the air. His wife had made breakfast, that much was obvious. As he climbed out of bed, she appeared at the bedroom door, a white apron tied at the waist of her sky blue morning dress.

"Good morning, Jonathan."

A smile blossomed on his lips. Everyone else in the world called him Jon, but she was different. She always called him Jonathan. So formal, and yet somehow it sounded appropriate coming from her lips. It seemed to make her more feminine, more desirable. It made him feel special.

"Good morning, Alice."

She stepped closer, they embraced and kissed.

"Breakfast is ready," she said unnecessarily. "Are you hungry?"

"I am now, I smelt the bacon."

"We're also having pancakes with fresh apple butter…or maple syrup if you prefer." She embellished a toothy grin. "Would you like some coffee?"

"I'll have everything you're making," he told her.

She kissed him again, started to leave, but didn't get very far when he reached out and grabbed her from behind, bringing her back. She giggled.

"My God, Jonathan, we don't have time for this!"

He refused to let go as she wriggled to break free. Finally she gave up and relaxed in his arms.

"That's better," he said, and kissed her on the mouth.

"A beautiful morning it is, darling."

He glanced at the window behind them, where a thin

streak of cornflower blue showed through a rift in the curtains. Just like the color of his wife's lovely eyes.

"I'm going to need more firewood for the stove," she told him.

"I'll take care of it later."

He released her and lay back on the bed, pillowing his head in his hands. He watched as she stepped over to the window and opened the curtains wider. He squinted as the sunlight poured into the room.

"Today is our last day together," he said, snaring her attention. "Tomorrow I'll be in Harrisburg. By Monday I'll be back with my regiment in Virginia."

"How much longer will the war go on, Jonathan?"

"Don't know, Alice. Maybe it'll be over by the time I leave in the morning. Wouldn't that be something?"

"It's so peaceful here," she said to the window. "One would never know there's a war going on in this country." She looked back, expecting him to say something, but he didn't. She shrugged and left the bedroom.

He waited a while longer before heaving himself out of bed. He stepped into his trousers, walked over to the window and peered out.

Yes, a beautiful morning indeed.

He spotted the apple orchard in the distance. About a quarter mile away, it was. An Amish farmer named Gross once owned the vast field of fruit trees. He remembered when he and his brother used to sneak into the orchard and stuff their pockets with ripe, juicy red apples. Old man Gross caught them one day performing their act of larceny and informed their dad. Not much later the spanking occurred. Jon smiled as he replayed the episode in his mind. Yes, he missed Peter, would miss him for the rest of his life.

Reluctantly he turned away from the window and brushed back the tear as it fell from his eye.

The following day was overcast and cool, with little wind and humidity as husband and wife stood side by side on the station platform.

Jon Westmoreland was in full uniform, including side arm and riding boots. His wife wore a blue dress and matching coat, a pink and yellow bonnet, and a black shawl wrapped snugly about her shoulders. There were six other couples waiting at the west end of the platform. All of the men were dressed in military garb, their spouses clinging to them like magnets. He wondered if they were all newlyweds too. He leaned down and kissed his wife on the forehead with affection.

"I'll write to you every week, Alice."

"I'll write to you every day," she said, fighting back the tears.

The passenger train, a plume of black smoke spewing from the steam engine, appeared and braked into the station. No one debarked. Men in army blue stared out at them from the open windows, their faces grim: the faces of men going to war. Jon glanced at his wife and frowned; she was crying. He opened his mouth as if to speak, but nothing came out from between his lips. Alice waited, wishing he would say something, but nothing continued to happen. She reached closer and stroked his face, wondering if she were seeing him for the last time. Then, suddenly, she broke free from his arms and scampered away, putting distance between them in a hurry. Captain Jonathan Westmoreland grabbed his gear and climbed aboard the train.

Sergeant-Major O'Grady couldn't get over the strange color in his beard. At the start of the war he was an incorrigible, stout, rock-faced man of twenty-nine, his dark beard a proud showpiece for both sexes to admire. Now, three and a half years later, he was still incorrigible, rock-faced and stout. The only thing different about him was his "pride 'n joy". It was flecked with gray, a sign that life had changed and would never be the same. He lowered the hand mirror and shook his head sadly.

Sean Michael O'Grady had joined the army straight out of the coal mines of central Pennsylvania. He knew very little about horses then, had hated them with fervor. He remembered it'd had something to do with their odor. He changed his opinion in a hurry at the stone bridge in Chattanooga, the day his scouting patrol was bushwhacked and he the only survivor.

He had been wounded in the right forearm by a rebel sharpshooter and left for dead when the young officer and his black stallion arrived on the scene. He remembered being shoved onto the saddle and told to hang on by the lieutenant as he spurred the horse into a gallop. Later at the field hospital, he passed out when the surgeon with the blood-stained smock began probing his wound with the metal "digger". When he had regained consciousness, the first thing he saw was the lieutenant's smiling face hovering above him.

His admiration for Jon Westmoreland escalated after that. They became very good friends, each one feeding on the other's field of expertise: O'Grady of the lieutenant's love of horses; Westmoreland of the sergeant's mastery of the carbine rifle. But there was more. There was mutual respect between them, the kind only brothers shared. They always looked out for each other.

O'Grady raised the mirror and studied the face staring back. Yes, he was older, perhaps with more color in his beard than he had expected at the age of thirty-two. But he was wiser too, much wiser. He had the captain to thank for that. And the war.

Rusty Jamison, the regimental runner, appeared in the duty tent, startling O'Grady. Customary of his personality, Jamison wore a sardonic grin that always seemed glued to his pimple-ridden face. It was the kind of smile that told the world he viewed life as one joke after another.

"Morning, Sergeant."

"Yes, Private, what is it?"

Jamison removed his cap, scratched a spot near the crest of his red-haired scalp, and said, "Thought you should know we got us a visitor."

"Oh, who is it this time?"

"Don't know his name, but he's an officer—a major. That much I do know."

O'Grady grunted. As usual, Jamison was playing games with him, something he was not in the mood for.

"All right, Rusty, out with it. Who is he and what does he want?"

"But I told you, I don't know his name. All I know is that he's looking for you."

"You must be daft. Majors don't go looking for sergeants, they have us sent for. Don't you know that by now?"

"But he's waiting outside. Think you better go out there. He don't look like a patient man."

O'Grady reached for his cap and left the duty tent at the march, Jamison right behind him. The visitor, standing near a dogwood tree, was smoking a hand-rolled cigar. O'Grady noted the man's rank; Jamison had not been kidding about that. He stepped closer with more alacrity, brought his boots together and saluted.

"Good morning, Major, my name is O'Grady. Understand you want to see me."

Joshua Stairs removed the cigar from his mouth.

"I've urgent business with Captain Westmoreland, Sergeant-Major. You know where I might find him?"

"Last I heard, he's due back at camp today, sir. Was away on furlough, you know. Went home to get hitched."

"No, I wasn't aware of that." Stairs' eyes wandered. "That's most troubling," he added, speaking to the tree.

"Beg pardon, sir?"

"Never mind, Sergeant, I'll be back." Stairs shoved the cigar in his mouth and walked away.

When he was out of earshot, Jamison said, "Now ain't that strange. What do you reckon he wants to see the captain for?"

"God knows. But you can bet your socks it ain't nothin'

good. Majors don't go looking for junior officers just for fun."

Jonathan Westmoreland arrived at the duty tent of the Thirteenth Pennsylvania Cavalry just before noon. O'Grady was the first to greet him and told him about the stone-faced major who had been there earlier.

"What did he want, Sean?"

"He didn't say, sir, but it must be important. Said he'd come back."

Just then Rusty Jamison appeared. The skinny redhead seemed in a huff about something, unlike his usual jocular self.

"Beg pardon, Cap'n."

"Yes, Private?"

"Thought you should know that major's on his way over here again. Be here any minute."

The three exited the tent and saw the major in the immaculate uniform approaching. Westmoreland felt the smile on his lips as he recognized his old friend. He and Joshua Stairs had served together at Vicksburg, were members of General Grant's personal staff the day the enemy surrendered the city. Westmoreland honored his friend with a smart salute, and Stairs reciprocated with the same one he had been using throughout the war.

"Good to see you again, Captain." Stairs' grin stretched from ear to ear as they shook hands.

"Forever is a long time since Vicksburg," Westmoreland told him. "What can I do for you, sir?"

"I need some of your time, Jon." Stairs said to O'Grady, "I need to speak to the captain in private, Sergeant-Major. See to it we're not disturbed."

"Yes, sir." O'Grady nudged Jamison with his elbow. "Let's go, Rusty," and they left at the march.

Inside the duty tent, Stairs produced a crumpled map from his coat pocket, spread it out across the table and started the briefing.

III

"So there it is, Captain." Stairs leaned back from the map table. "What do you think?"

Westmoreland pursed his lips and deliberated. To Stairs, he seemed unsure of himself, as though struggling to find the right words to answer. The defining clue was the solemn, ash-colored mood on his face.

"I once met General Lee," he said finally. "It was during my second year at the Point. He was making an inspection tour." Westmoreland offered his friend a faint smile, though his eyes were somewhere else. "We shook hands," he added.

"Yes, I know all about that, Jon. But this mission will go

ahead as planned. We've no other choice."

"But assassinating a human being is like shooting a dumb animal. General Lee deserves a better fate than that. How could General Grant order you to do this?"

"In fact, it was the president who gave the general full authority to proceed."

"President Lincoln?"

"Yes. He knows it's the best, the quickest way to save lives in the field. He wants this war ended now, Captain, not tomorrow."

Westmoreland shook his head, was still in disbelief of everything he had heard. Hands on the table, he dropped his chin and restudied the map. Stairs noted the gold wedding ban on his ring finger and remembered the words of his boss.

"I can't order you to do this, Jon. The general wants volunteers only, preferably unmarried men. And that includes you."

Westmoreland's face showed a picture of surprise.

"You knew I was married?"

"Yes, the sergeant told me all about it." Smiling, Stairs clapped him on the shoulder. "Congratulations."

"Thanks, Josh."

Stairs returned to the main topic when he said, "You're the best man for the job, Captain. I know it and the general knows it. But if you want to back out, just say the word."

"You said I could pick my own men?"

"Yes, but they've got to be the best you can muster. The best riders, the best marksmen."

"The toughest part of your plan will be to breach the

enemy pickets near Richmond."

"I receive daily reports on where the enemy lines are weakest," Stairs assured him. "I'll make sure you get the latest reconnaissance before you leave. Like I said before, this will be a hit-and-run raid—a mission of stealth. You must avoid contact with the enemy at all costs."

"But if we're spotted, the Rebs will track us down like a pack of starving wolves. We'll be lucky to get back."

"And if you don't, it's prison camp for the lot of you. Not a pleasant prospect, I admit."

"So when do we leave?"

"The day after tomorrow," was Stairs' reply. "However, if you want to back out, tell me now. Volunteers only for this job."

Westmoreland hesitated, thinking about what he would do, then started a slow pacing routine, back and forth like a caged lion. But it didn't last long.

"Josh, I've only been married a short time. When the war's over, Alice and I are going to start a family. But it's hard to forget the others who died in this war fighting for our country. Many were married men with families. If I had children, I might say no, but I don't."

"Then...you'll do it?"

"Yes, Major, I'll do it. The president was right, this war must be ended."

"We've been through a helluva lot together, Jon. Shiloh, Vicksburg, Chattanooga. I was there when General Grant awarded you the Medal of Honor." He smiled. "Remember?"

"Yes, I remember."

Stairs carried on, "If anyone can succeed, it's you, Captain. In fact, I'll bet my next pay you make it back alive. However, if things go wrong and you're unable to complete your mission, you have the option to turn back and save your men."

Westmoreland had nothing more to say, just watched as his friend donned his cap and left the duty tent. A minute later O'Grady appeared.

"Well, Jon, what's it all about?"

"We're going for a horse ride, Sergeant-Major."

"Reconnaissance, sir?"

"No, not this time." Westmoreland's eyes were piercing swords as he continued, "Five men, Sean, I need five good men—all volunteers. And they must be crack shots and ride like the wind."

O'Grady thought. Not much later he was ready.

"Jake Carson, Shorty Jones…and Billy Flanagan," he said, counting with his fingers. "Those three will volunteer for anything. And they're all dead shots too. Then there's Corporal Greene. You know what he can do with a rifle." O'Grady smiled proudly. "And me makes five."

"Any of them married?"

"Just Greene, sir."

"Does he have any children?"

"Yeah, two little ones, I think."

"Then he can't go."

O'Grady's face wrinkled into a mask of confusion. His eyes showed the same mood.

"Beg pardon, Cap'n, but you're married."

Westmoreland ignored him.

"You'll have to find another man, Sergeant."

"Yes, sir."

"Very well, dismissed."

When he was gone, Westmoreland looked down at the map and forced himself to concentrate on the new task awaiting him. Only it didn't work. His eyes ached, and the pounding inside his forehead was merciless. He cleared his thoughts—it did work—and saw the image of two people, a man and a woman, pop into his head. The couple was engaged in passionate love-making of the unrelenting kind, just as it had been on their wedding night. Then, suddenly, the picture of his wife and her husband faded into the darkness of his memory. Jon Westmoreland sighed and made a decision.

Time to write a letter.

As it turned out, the man O'Grady found to replace Greene was unmarried and childless. But Zachary Miller enjoyed the company of women, perhaps more so than he cared to admit. He remembered when he had nearly tied the knot. The girl was a bounty of beauty: flowing, straw blond hair; succulent lips the color of cherries; and more than enough bosom to keep him happy for a lifetime. The problem was that she was only fifteen years old. They planned to elope and never return, which seemed like a good idea until the soon-to-be father of the bride got wind of the plan two days in advance. The old man went berserk and chased after the hopeful bridegroom with a hunting rifle, which to Miller looked like a cannon. In the end the wedding was postponed and never rescheduled.

But Zack Miller's favorite thing to do was drink. "Drink like there's no tomorrow," he had been heard to say on several occasions. At that moment Miller was involved in loud, passionate slumber, sleeping off what had been a rambunctious night of guzzling beer, crude-tasting distilled whiskey, and other spirits he and his drinking buddies had been able to get their hands on. O'Grady frowned with distaste as he stared down at the prostrate figure of Miller lying on the camp bed. His snoring routine reminded the sergeant-major of a saw going through dry oak.

"How long's he been like that?" he asked the soldier standing beside him.

"Since early this morning," replied Billy Flanagan. "Zack really tied one on this time, didn't he? Hell, you couldn't wake him with artillery fire."

"All right, Corporal, light a match."

"But, Sergeant, you don't mean—"

"Damn right I do!"

Flanagan struck a match and placed it under Miller's bare right foot. Nothing happened.

"Closer," O'Grady told him.

"But, Sean, I'll burn his foot off."

"Don't jaw with me, Billy. Do it!"

Flanagan did so, and the inevitable followed. Miller spasmed in earthquake fashion and leaped out of the bed shouting obscenities. He hopped around on his left foot to ease the pain in the other, but then lost his balance and fell, ending up in a twisted pile on the floor. Foul words still gushing from his mouth, he squeezed his eyes shut and waited impatiently for the pain in his foot to fade into the past. When he reopened them, he saw the blurred faces of Flanagan and O'Grady staring down at him. The former was smiling; the latter was not.

"What in the name of John Brown!" Miller blinked furiously, and the two soldiers came into focus. "Is that you, Sergeant…Billy?"

"On your feet!" commanded O'Grady.

Miller stood up groggily and somehow kept himself there. His uniform reeked with the stale scent of last night.

"I don't get it," he mumbled, "what happened to the girl?"

"Girl! What girl?" O'Grady snarled at him. "What the hell you talkin' about?"

"The girl, Sergeant, she was here a minute ago." Miller gingerly touched his forehead. It felt loose from the constant spinning inside, as though it were about to fall off. "Who hit me with a shovel?"

"He's still drunk," said Flanagan, chuckling between words.

O'Grady said, "You're a disgrace to the uniform, Corporal Miller."

"I know I done wrong, Sergeant, but…" Miller stared at O'Grady with wide eyes begging for mercy. "You ain't gonna tell the captain, are you?" His voice was terrified.

Ignoring him, O'Grady said to Flanagan, "Pump him full of black coffee. If that don't work, try a jar of molasses."

"If I wasn't in a good mood, I'd ask the captain to put you on report," O'Grady told Miller later that day after the latter had sobered up. "How many times you done this to me before? Hell, I lost count!"

"But you need me, Sergeant." Miller glanced at Flanagan. "Ain't that right, Billy?"

"Drunk or sober, Zack's the best shot in the regiment, Sean."

"I once shot the tail off a buck without drawing blood," said Miller proudly. "Ain't that right, Billy?"

"So what?" growled O'Grady. "What you need is a lesson in army discipline."

"Oh, no! Please, Sergeant, don't put me on mess duty again. I hate peelin' them damn spuds. I'll do anything but that, anything!"

O'Grady made no comment in return, enjoying watching the man squirm. Flanagan was also enjoying his performance.

He said, "I got an idea, Sergeant. Zack could spit-shine all the officers' boots."

"No, I got a better idea," countered O'Grady. "He can polish *all* the boots in the regiment."

"No, Sarge!" pleaded Miller.

"Sergeant-Major to you," O'Grady corrected him.

"Please, don't do that to me. That's gotta be…a hundred boots, for God's sake."

"A hundred and eighty-four pair to be exact," said the grinning Flanagan.

Miller swallowed the knot in his throat.

"Sergeant-Major, please, you and me is best friends, ain't we?"

"All right, Corporal Miller, here's what you're gonna do.

As of now you're the new company runner. Anything that needs to be done, you get the job." O'Grady pushed his angry face within an inch of Miller's pale one. "Got that, soldier?"

"Thank you! Thank you, Sergeant-Major!"

"One more thing, Zack, you gotta stay sober. If I find out you been drinkin' again, you'll be Private Miller faster than you can sing 'Camp Town Races'. Got it?"

"Yes, Sergeant-Major, you got my word of honor." Miller smiled bravely, showing a mouthful of neglected teeth. "Now 'bout that horse ride you was talkin' about. When do we leave?"

"You'll know that when I do," O'Grady told him.

IV

The summer and early autumn of 1864 had brought tremendous hardship to the Confederacy. Perhaps hardest hit was the Commonwealth of Virginia, where the bulk of the fighting was taking place, and the price of food and other essentials needed to survive was beyond the means of most residents and their families, including the wealthy. Goods from overseas had ceased to exist due to the Federal blockades, and when Sherman split the South in half following his methodical, blood-stained march to the sea, most realized that final defeat was just around the corner.

George Bailey, a Richmond native and owner of the

Sweetwater Tavern on Locust Street, had known the end was near after learning the tragic news of the Confederate defeat at Gettysburg. Bailey lost three cousins and a brother-in-law during the battle. From that day on the standard of living in the great state began its rapid decline.

It started with the inflated price of sugar and bread, then bacon. Coffee and tea soon became rare commodities, along with milk, eggs, butter and honey. Bailey's liquor stock had dwindled—he was compelled to construct a homemade distillery—and he stayed in business only because his patrons, of whom most were invalided war veterans, paid him in Yankee greenbacks, money confiscated from captured Union soldiers on their way to the city's prisoner detention camps. A man of means, Bailey was preparing for the future.

The night before he'd had a lengthy discussion with his wife about the war, in particular the blundering administration in charge of running it. "Jeff Davis is a cold-hearted idiot," he told her. "It's time to stop the war before there ain't nothin' left."

Dorothy Bailey just shrugged in response, her jaded eyes showing no feelings for his words, as though he didn't exist. Not that it mattered, for she was dying in a hurry, had been for several months due to a stomach cancer. "The mystery disease," the doctor had called it.

Unbeknownst to her, her husband was planning for that eventuality too. He had already taken a mistress. She was five years his senior, a wide, buxom woman whose looks had since deserted her and whose husband, a wealthy infantry officer, had taken a shot between the eyes at Chancellorsville not far from where Stonewall Jackson had met his demise. But that was war, and he, George Bailey, more than anything else he was, was a man of means.

The Sweetwater Tavern was empty that night except for Bailey and his lone customer, who was sitting slumped over the counter at the far end of the bar. It had been a slow business night, barely worth his time to stay open. He had just wiped down the bar and was sweeping out the place when the front door opened with a bang.

The first man who stepped in with the butternut uniform and crooked stride was his close friend and neighbor, Skip Davison, who lived just across the street from the tavern. Davison was a large man with a long gray beard, and the permanent limp he brought with him was his legacy at Culp's Hill on that infamous third day at the Gettysburg battlefield.

The second one through the portal was another of Bailey's regular patrons. Nats Parker was a feisty, sixty-nine-year-old carpenter of snow-white hair and spectacles who had known Bailey's father and his before him. He had helped build the Sweetwater with his own hands a half century earlier, a fact he was most proud of and had reminded Bailey on several occasions.

"Was just fixin' to close," Bailey told them.

"Horse dung!" fired back Davison. "Nats and me is thirsty. And don't tell us you're fresh out 'cause I smelt your still cookin' three blocks away."

Davison punctuated his words with sarcastic laughter, and Parker said, "That's right, Georgie. Let's have some of that real whiskey you hide under the bar."

"Whiskey!" Bailey frowned. "What whiskey you talkin' about?"

"The kind that's gonna take the pain out of my leg," said Davison. He plopped his rump on the stool in front of Bailey. "My God, that's better. One of these days I reckon my leg's gonna fall off."

Bailey placed three tumblers on the bar, produced the whiskey bottle and poured equal portions for each of them. Parker grabbed his drink first and finished it in one swallow.

"Another, Georgie," he said with a toothless grin.

"Not till I see some Yankee money in front of me," Bailey told him.

"They could hang you fer that," snarled Parker. "Everybody knows what you're doing."

Bailey ignored him.

"On the bar, old man. No money, no whiskey."

"Don't get the dander up, Georgie." Parker drove his hand deep into his hip pocket and reluctantly slapped two bits on the counter. "Happy now?"

"Nats is right," said Davison, lending his opinion. "They can hang you from a tree for what you been doing."

"So what?" argued Bailey. "I ain't done nothin' no one else ain't. I'm just looking out for my interests. A man's gotta make a living, ain't he? And since our government money ain't worth nothin' no more, I'm taking anything that comes along. Just last week Major Hawkins paid me in gold. Another fellow come in here one night and give me a pocket watch for a glass of my homemade liquor. Can you believe it?"

They laughed. Then Davison changed the subject.

"How's the wife, Georgie? Feeling any better?"

"Nope, she's worse. Doc Benjamin says she ain't got no more than a week or two left."

"Which don't bother you a'tall, do it?" said Parker with noticeable sarcasm. Then quickly added, "Don't worry, Georgie, everybody knows 'bout that Montgomery widow woman you been takin' up with."

"Ain't there nothing you don't know about me, old man?"

"Nope, nothing." Parker put the tumbler to his lips, drank, and then heaved himself off the stool. "Well, I'm feeling my age. See you round, boys."

The door closed behind him, and Davison said, "That old bastard, wonder when he's gonna croak. Soon, I hope. I'm tired of hearin' him bellyachin' all the time. Ain't nothin' but a dirty old man. Knows everybody's business."

"Who cares?" Bailey poured. "Have another, Skip."

"Much obliged, Georgie." Davison emptied his tumbler too fast and coughed. "You know, I'm getting tired of nothing to do. Know what I mean?"

"When the war's over, come work for me, Skip. You can tend bar, if you have a mind to."

"Nope, don't want it. That's work for a darkie, not a white man."

They chuckled.

Davison swung his attention to the man sitting slumped at the other end of bar. He reckoned him to be a young man, although his head was turned the other way and resting on his arms. His hair was dirty blond, and the clothes on his person looked store-bought new.

"Who's him, Georgie? Don't think I know him."

"That's Billy Joe Eldridge, my old lady's nephew."

"Looks like he's dead."

"No, just tired."

"A young stud like that ought to be in uniform," said Davison, fondling his tumbler. "Everybody I know done his share in the war."

"Reckon he's on furlough."

Davison was skeptical and showed it in his bloodshot eyes.

"Come on, Georgie, what gives? Who is he?"

"I told you, his name is Billy Joe Eldridge."

"He's a deserter, ain't he? That's why he ain't in uniform."

Bailey squirmed, aware he was on slippery ground.

"All right, if you gotta know, he went over the hill 'bout a month back. For God's sake, Skip, he's just a boy, not even seventeen yet. He don't belong in the war."

"That ain't for you to say, Georgie. They could hang him for deserting."

"Not if nobody finds him." Bailey winked at his friend, but there was no reaction from the big man. He went on, "Billy Joe's my wife's only living nephew. I want him to take over the business when they drop me in the box. Hell, you know I ain't got no kin. He already lost his old man and big brother in the war. That's enough for one family, ain't it?"

"Reckon you're right, Georgie. Guess I'm just bitter 'bout the way things happened to me. My leg ain't never gonna be the same." He shook his head with emphasis. "This damned war!"

"It should've ended a long time ago," added Bailey with

disgust. "Look at the awful mess we're in. Somebody ought to hang Jeff Davis for what he done to Virginia. We're gonna lose the war, that's a fact. Those damn Yankees will come here and take all we got. We'll be lucky if they let us keep our names."

"If we could just get rid of old Bobby Lee when he gets here next week, maybe it might bust up the army. He's the one holding it together, you know."

"Next week!" Bailey frowned. "What do you mean, Skip? What's this 'bout General Lee?"

"You don't know?"

"Know what?" Bailey poured. "Tell me."

"It's just a rumor goin' round." Davison reached for his tumbler, and Bailey became impatient.

"Come on, Skip, tell me."

Davison drank, grimaced when the hot liquor settled in his stomach, and said, "I heared General Lee is coming to the city next week to see the president."

"What for?"

"Don't know, Georgie. But if I was to take a guess, I'd say he's coming to beg for more troops. Why else would he come?"

"Who told you this, Skip?"

"Nats."

"How does he know?"

"That old bastard knows everything."

"No, he don't, someone told him." Bailey leaned closer. "Who was it?"

"Reckon it was his grandson, Virgil," was Davison's reply.

"He's a hash slinger for the Virginia Ninth, my old regiment. He heared some officers talkin' about General Lee coming here next week to see the president."

"Is that so?" Bailey pondered. "Tell me more, Skip."

Davison told his friend what he knew, including the fact that Lee would be making several stops on the return trip. One included a visit to the army hospital in Willistown, a spit in the road just twenty-five miles southeast of Richmond.

"Well, if that don't beat all," said Bailey when he had finished.

"I'm plum tuckered out." Davison emptied his tumbler and slid off the stool, moaning like a sick mule as he put pressure on the bad leg. "Thanks for the whiskey, Georgie. Reckon I'll be able to sleep tonight for a change. Be seein' ya."

Davison glanced back at Billy Joe, as if ready to say something, but somehow refrained from doing so. He shook his head and limped toward the exit.

When he was gone, Bailey made a decision. He walked to the end of the bar and tapped his wife's nephew on the shoulder, rousing him.

"Billy Joe, wake up!"

The young man raised his head slowly and squinted at Bailey.

"Uncle George?" He blinked furiously, adjusting his eyes to the light in the room. "What is it, sir?"

"Listen to me, Billy Joe, and listen good."

"What is it? Are they looking fer me, Uncle George?" His voice was terrified.

"No, they ain't," Bailey assured him. "Now listen to me,

boy, I got a job for you. Remember when you run away from the army? Well, you're gonna do it again."

"But they'll hang me, Uncle George! They'll hang me fer sure!"

"No, they won't, 'cause they won't find you."

"But I can't do it! I don't wanna!"

"Look, boy, you're goin' over the hill again, only this time you're gonna do it different. You're gonna give yourself up to the Yankee army."

Billy Joe's eyes were clogged with a mixture of confusion and fear.

"But they'll chuck me in prison camp!" He shook his head defiantly. "No, I don't wanna go. They say the fellows there eat rats. I hate rats, Uncle George, I hate 'em!"

"Look, boy, if you stay here someone's bound to see you and turn you in. When that happens, they'll come looking for me. Besides, what I got in mind is gonna make you a hero."

"Hero?"

"Yeah, I got important information that's gonna save Virginia. And you're gonna take it to the Yankee army."

"But how, Uncle George? How…do I get through the Yankee pickets?"

"There's always a way to get through."

"But I'll need a horse, sir. You know I ain't got none."

"I'll get you a horse, don't you worry, boy."

"But I don't get it. What am I gonna do, just give myself up when I reach the Yankee pickets?"

"Yep, that's exactly what you're gonna do."

"But what do I tell 'em, Uncle George? What kind

of…important information you got that's gonna make me a hero?"

Bailey told him.

V

Peter Wilson was a veteran infantryman. A second generation American who had run away from home to join the army, he was a cocksure twenty-two-year-old when armed conflict broke out between North and South. Like many his age, he regarded the war as a once-in-a-lifetime enterprise of fun and adventure. His attitude took a different path in the first summer of the war following the Federal rout at Manassas Junction, where nearly twenty percent of his regiment made the ultimate sacrifice and the balance retreated in pell-mell disgrace. From that point on, his lust for excitement and glory became a simple matter of survival.

But Pete Wilson was committed to his duty, his president and his country. After his two-year hitch was up, he reenlisted to the surprise of his comrades, of whom many were destined for home to mend what was left of their shattered lives. Despite his personal feelings about the war, Wilson had proved his worth many times over as a leader in the Sixth New Hampshire Volunteers. Along with his usual duties, he was entrusted with the thankless job of training new recruits, boys who quickly learned to appreciate his expertise as a veteran of four major campaigns. That is, if they wanted to survive.

The air was cool that Tuesday morning, the dew on the ground a frosty glaze as the lanky sergeant from Hanover came awake to the sound of his own name. Wilson blinked and saw Corporal Hardy Jenkins staring down at him, concern attached to his homely face. Wilson frowned back with noticeable disdain.

"What is it, Hardy? What are you doing to me?"

"Sorry to rouse you, Sergeant, but we got us another rabbit."

Wilson rolled out of the bed with reluctance and gently stroked his handlebar moustache, making sure it was there.

"Where is this Johnny Reb?"

"Outside the mess tent with Charlie and Skeeter," was Jenkins' reply. "They give him some hot sausage and cornbread to eat. Charlie says he come through the pickets 'bout an hour a'fore the sun come up." He chuckled. "That makes nine of 'em the past three days."

"I lost count." Wilson took a short moment to scratch the

stubble under his chin, just above the Adam's apple. "Does the lieutenant know yet?"

"No, Pete."

Wilson thought. Just what he needed, another Reb prisoner to nurse maid. Only what was he going to do with him? The tents were already overcrowded.

"Okay, Hardy, let's go see the new rabbit. Maybe the lieutenant will know what to do with him."

The rabbit, formally known as Billy Joe Eldridge, had been apprehended earlier that morning by a foot patrol just nineteen miles southeast of Richmond, roughly a mile west of the Sixth New Hampshire pickets. None of the Yankees present was surprised by the young man's sudden arrival, for they had captured scores of enemy deserters the past three months. What baffled them was the young man's appearance: the clean uniform he wore; the soled shoes that looked new; and a slender body that seemed fit and well-nourished.

Sitting under a red maple, back propped against the trunk, Billy Joe watched with interest as Wilson and Jenkins approached. Since his capture, Dorothy Bailey's nephew had been treated with kindness and respect. They had fed him well too. The sausage was plump and juicy, and the coffee was real, something he had not tasted before or after deserting his post three weeks previous.

"He ain't no older than my kid brother," said Wilson, staring down at Billy Joe. "Is that the best the Reb army can do?"

"Yeah, he's still gotta be wearing his three-corner pants,"

said Jenkins, chuckling between words. "Hell, Pete, I doubt he knows one end of a rifle from t'other. Why don't we turn him loose? We sure ain't got no room for him."

Before Wilson could respond, Billy Joe said, "Reckon I wouldn't do that if I was you, Corporal."

Jenkins' jaw dropped like a rock from the sky, evidence that he was startled by the boy's curious choice of words. Wilson, wearing a similar look, crouched beside the prisoner.

"What's your name, Johnny Reb?"

"Billy Joe."

"Billy Joe what?"

"Billy Joe Eldridge."

"Where you from?"

"Richmond."

"Is that so?" Wilson pondered. "All right, boy, tell me, why can't we let you go?"

"'Cause I can make you famous, Sergeant."

Wilson burst into a thunderclap of laughter.

"Go on, Johnny Reb, I'm all ears. Tell me about it."

Billy Joe explained. When he had finished reciting his uncle's important information, Wilson offered no hint of emotion, nor made any effort to challenge the validity of the young man's narrative. Jenkins, though, reacted in a different manner.

"That's the biggest fairy tale lie I ever heared," he said to Wilson. "Think we gave the boy too much coffee and sugar."

Wilson said to the prisoner, "Where did you get this story 'bout General Lee?"

Billy Joe told him.

Jenkins said, "For heaven's sake, Pete, you don't believe him, do you?"

"I don't know what to believe, Hardy. But say the kid's telling the truth. Think what would happen if we was able to kill Lee."

"Ah, that's crazy, Sergeant, and you know it."

"Maybe. But if we did kill him, we *would* be famous, like the kid said. Don't you wanna be famous, Hardy?"

"He's right, Corporal," cut in Billy Joe. "You'll be so famous, I reckon they'll write stories about you after the war. Maybe carve a statue with your face on it."

"Why, so the pigeons can crap on me?" Jenkins laughed again, but Wilson did not participate.

He said, "I'm gonna tell the lieutenant about this."

"But he'll just laugh at you, Sergeant."

Lieutenant Bernard Woodside did indeed laugh after Wilson had delivered the information to him later that morning. Before long the laughter subsided, and Woodside decided it would be prudent of him to reassess Bill Joe's story before passing final judgment. He removed his cap and scratched the back of his head with care.

"What's your opinion, Sergeant?"

"Don't know, Lieutenant. Could be this Johnny Reb's pulling our legs. Could be he hates Lee for some reason or t'other. Or maybe he said it just to get special treatment. Like hot food and a soft bed."

"Yeah, maybe you're right. Besides, what difference does it make? Even if we knew where Lee was, we'd never get close enough to shoot him."

"You know that for a fact, sir?"

"No, of course I don't," muttered the sullen Woodside.

"So what you gonna do, Lieutenant?"

"Well, I'm obliged to report this—it's part of my job. But I doubt the colonel will do anything about it. However, I must admit, it's fodder for thought."

"What do you mean?"

"Well, say we did kill Lee. Who would believe it might end the war?" Woodside shook his head, then answered his own question. "No, no one would, I tell you. In fact, if you put that idea to General Grant himself, he'd only laugh in your face."

Just seven miles away, Sean O'Grady stuck the chew of tobacco in his mouth, leaned over the table and studied the map. He had listened to the plan attentively, without uttering a solitary word in rebuttal. Not a peep out of him, observed Westmoreland.

"You've been awfully quiet, Sergeant-Major. Tell me, what are you thinking?"

"With all due respect to Major Stairs, I think his plan smells," was O'Grady's terse response.

"Oh, any particular reason why?"

"Yes, sir. First we gotta get through the Reb pickets. That means we gotta cross the river. And you know what that's gonna be like. If we do make it across, we can't get spotted."

"Go on."

"Well, say we make it across. Then we gotta find the best

way to hit the target. And that means we gotta get close, *real* close."

"Was thinking of that, Sean. I believe I have the solution. We'll use a diversion."

"Diversion, sir?"

"That's right. It will throw the enemy off guard and allow one of us to sneak in and shoot Lee."

"Who was you thinkin' about, Jon? Miller's the best shot in the regiment."

"No, it will have to be me."

O'Grady squinted at his friend, not liking what he had heard. He leaned away from the map table, bent down and spat used tobacco into the spittoon beside him. He wiped the dribble from his chin with his sleeve.

"Beg pardon, Cap'n, but I don't like it, not one damned bit. You'll only get one shot at Lee, maybe two if you're lucky. After that the Rebs will swarm round you like bees to a honeycomb. You'll never get away. Did you think about that?"

"Of course."

"But, Jon, don't you think it would be better to use all of us? Concentrated fire, I mean."

"Then no one gets back alive. No, they'll hang us, Sean, you know it and I know it. My duty is to get all of you back one way or another."

"But, Cap'n, what about you? Hell, this ain't nothin' but a suicide mission. Ain't no glory in it for nobody. I get a sour taste in my mouth just thinkin' about it."

"I know what you mean, Sergeant. I once met General

Lee. I have much respect for him."

"Then get out of it, sir. Get out while you can before it's too late."

"No, I've already given my word to Major Stairs."

"But it's suicide, Jon!"

"Perhaps, but the war's got to end. General Grant wants it to end now. And if he believes that killing Lee will accomplish that, then I'm all for it. Besides, if the situation were reversed, Lee would no doubt try to do the same to him."

"So when you gonna tell the others?"

"Soon. If they don't like what they hear, they can back out."

"Well, I can promise you one thing, Cap'n, none of 'em will back out." O'Grady grinned. "They'll follow you into hell."

O'Grady was right about that.

"We'll take enough rations for three days," Westmoreland told them after he had outlined the plan later in the day. "After that we'll have to live off the land."

"Why three days, Cap'n?" The question belonged to Jake Carson. "Are you wantin' to take the long way back?"

"A fair question, Corporal, but we're not coming back."

O'Grady said, "Beg pardon, sir, but what the hell you talkin' about?"

"Listen to me—all of you. If we're successful, the Rebs will expect us to retreat the way we came in. My idea is to outfox the hound." Westmoreland drew an imaginary line on the map with his index finger. "We'll head due east."

"East, sir?" queried a confused Miller.

"That's right, Zack. It's the best, the only way back."

VI

*A*lmighty and most merciful Lord, I have endured the privations and horrors of this war on behalf of my beloved homeland. I have witnessed the sight of many good men fighting and dying for the cause. Help me now that I might find wisdom and strength to continue the battles to come.

Robert E. Lee opened his eyes and sighed with feeling. Yes, a cause for which there seemed no hope, and yet the war dragged on day after bloody day, with no end in sight. When it was over, he and he alone would be held accountable for the decisions which had prolonged the many years of suffering. Would he be forgiven in time in the eyes of man?

More importantly, would Almighty God forgive him?

The great man with the tangled beard of silver and white donned his spectacles. He stared at the casualty report he had received just moments earlier regarding the Cedar Creek engagement, which had ended in victory for the enemy. A long list indeed, and yet there were faces behind those names: faces of brave soldiers, the young and the veteran, of whom many had given the supreme sacrifice. Lee removed his spectacles and took a moment to massage his tired, aching eyes. If only there was a way to end the bloodshed...

Robert Edward Lee was born and bred to live the life of a soldier. It had started with his father, "Lighthorse" Harry Lee, a hero of the Revolution who was a close friend of George Washington, and later governor of Virginia. As a member of the Continental Congress, Robert's father had vigorously sponsored ratification of the most important document in American history—the Constitution. Despite his irrefutable loyalty as a public servant, Henry Lee made some rather poor financial decisions through the years which left his family near the brink of poverty. As a result, his son grew up with little more than his proud family heritage.

Robert entered the United States Military Academy at West Point and graduated in 1829 with the rank of second lieutenant. Two years later he married Mary Anne Randolph Custis, great-granddaughter of Martha Washington, in Arlington, Virginia. In the years that followed, he was assigned to engineering duties, some of which included overseeing needed improvements along the Mississippi River. Then the Mexican War happened, during which Captain Lee served as a staff officer under General Winfield Scott and experienced the grand victories at Vera Cruz and Chapultepec Castle. Other notables who served with him in Mexico included George B. McClellan, Thomas "Stonewall" Jackson, Joseph E. Johnston and George Gordon Meade.

After the Mexican War, Lee returned to his engineering duties and was responsible for the erection of Fort Carroll at Baltimore. Following his three-year tenure as superintendent of West Point, he was appointed lieutenant-colonel of the Second United States Cavalry by Jefferson Davis, who was secretary of war in President Franklin Pierce's cabinet. This afforded him the opportunity to serve in the Indian country, then later in Texas.

On 16 October 1859, the abolitionist John Brown, along with eighteen followers, seized control of the Federal armory at Harpers Ferry, Virginia. In the process, five civilians were killed and hostages taken. To repress the insurrection, Colonel Lee was ordered to Harpers Ferry where he took command of a detachment of marines dispatched from the Washington Navy Yard. During the ensuing action, the marines captured Brown, who had barricaded himself in an old engine house, and killed ten of his zealots, including two of his sons.

The country, now politically torn between North and South on the issue of slavery, was on the brink of collapse. Lee, who was against slavery, disfavored southern secession, and had no partiality for political extremists of either side, hoped the country would mend itself before armed conflict erupted. But by then it was too late; the die had been cast. Robert E. Lee, after thirty-two years of dedicated service in the military of his forbearers, had to choose between taking supreme command of the Union army and defending his beloved Virginia. In the end, his fateful decision of honor would make him a legend, and yet haunt him until his death.

The commander-in-chief of the Confederate Army of Northern Virginia smiled as Colonel Walter Taylor, his trusted aide-de-camp, entered the command hut, came to attention and saluted. Despite his youth, Taylor had aged far beyond his years. A result of the war, Lee knew. He acknowledged Taylor with a nod.

"Yes, Colonel?"

"Sorry to disturb you, General, but I was hoping to retire early this evening. Is there anything more you require of me?"

"You are not feeling well?"

"No, sir, I'm very well, thank you. Just tired, I reckon."

"Before you leave, Colonel, I understand we'll be making a stop in Willistown after our stay in Richmond."

"That's right, General. If you recall, you asked me to arrange it while we were having supper. Three nights ago, I believe it was. You said you wanted to visit the hospital there."

"Of course, please forgive me for the oversight."

"No need to apologize, sir. I'd have been astonished had you remembered everything on the itinerary."

"Very well, Colonel, please feel free to retire. And thank you for your help today. Hope I've not been more of a burden than usual."

"On the contrary, General, it's been my privilege."

"I pray that tomorrow will be a better day." Lee tendered a

grin. "Sleep well."

"And you, sir. I'll see you first thing in the morning."

Taylor brought his heels together and saluted. Lee answered the gesture with a nod and watched his aide leave the room. Not much later he heard a familiar voice in his mind.

What would I do without him?

Jonathan Westmoreland did not sleep well that night. The idea of what he was about to embark upon gnawed at him, like an itch he couldn't reach. He kept reminding himself of his duty, and yet killing a man he admired did not make sense. Would he actually go through with it? Could he look Lee in the eye when the moment came and squeeze the trigger? And how would posterity judge him? In the eyes of the North he would be branded a hero, in the South a demon. And what about the reputation of his family?

He awoke the next day with the same thoughts pestering him. He tried having fried eggs and buttered muffins for breakfast, but it didn't work. The coffee he was able to keep down even tasted bland. Sean O'Grady, who joined him after breakfast, noticed his grim demeanor at once.

"Bad night, Jon?"

"Yes, more so than usual."

"The boys are eager to get started, Cap'n. Guess they're itching for something to do." Westmoreland said nothing in return, and O'Grady switched topics. "Ain't had much time to thank you, Jon. That is, for all your help."

"What do you mean?"

"For saving my skin at Chattanooga, sir. I owe you my life."

"The way I remember it, I was doing the army a favor, Sergeant-Major."

O'Grady smiled as that day of two years ago in Tennessee flashed through his mind. He could still feel the searing pain in his arm as the hot mini ball from the sniper's rifle cut a hole in his flesh. He didn't notice the blood until Westmoreland pulled him out of the road and heaved him onto the saddle. By then his arm had gone numb, but he didn't pass out. That came later at the field hospital.

"Jon, do you believe we'll accomplish our mission? Do you believe killing Lee will end the war? Do you believe we'll all get back alive? Do you believe—"

"Slow down, Sean, one question at a time."

"Sorry, sir, but I been thinkin' about this a lot. I can't help but wonder—"

"I know, Sergeant, so have I. And I know exactly what you mean. But I don't have any answers for your questions. 'Fraid we'll just have to take our chances, do our best and hope we succeed."

"What about you, sir? Why did you choose to go along? You're married, for Pete's sake. You didn't gotta do it. All you had to do was say no to that major. You said yourself you respected Lee."

"Yes, but I gave Major Stairs my word. I'm indebted to him, as I am to General Grant and President Lincoln."

"The president, sir?" O'Grady's round face fractured into a frown of bewilderment. "Not sure I understand."

"The president wants this mission to succeed, Sean. It was he who gave the general authority to assassinate Lee."

"Golly!"

Westmoreland carried on, "The president believes that killing Lee will shorten the war, perhaps end it altogether. Can you imagine the burden he totes on his shoulders each day the war goes on?" He shook his head glumly. "No, I doubt anyone knows the answer to that."

"You're right," nodded O'Grady. "You're absolutely right."

Billy Joe Eldridge was scheduled to leave Virginia the next day, his destination an overcrowded prisoner-of-war camp near the industrial town of Dayton, Ohio. Within six months George Bailey's nephew by marriage would be dead from typhus, a fate that would befall twelve hundred other Confederate prisoners. Billy Joe would be remembered as a coward and not the hero his uncle had foreseen him to be.

His incredible story, however, had made its way to the commanding officer of the Sixth New Hampshire Regiment. At first, Colonel Thomas Pinckney listened to Woodside's report with reservations. Why would young Eldridge risk his life to tell such a fantastic story? Sure, the lad was a coward. Still...

He said to Woodside, "What do you make of this, Bernie?"

"Not sure, sir. The whole thing sounds preposterous."

"Come on, Lieutenant, I know you better than that. So out with it. What do you really think?"

"Well, Tom, say this Johnny Reb's telling the truth. Say Lee shows up where he's supposed to. What would it take to kill him?" Woodside paused for a breath of air, then answered his own question. "Well, I'll tell you, it would take a miracle."

"But what if it *was* possible?"

"But end the war?" Woodside grunted. "No, that I doubt, sir."

Pinckney made no effort to respond, and Woodside grew impatient.

"What are you going to do about this, Tom?"

Pinckney scratched the itch behind his ear and said, "Let's look at this logically, Bernie. Most Rebs who go over the hill are usually looking for a hot meal and dry bed. They're tired of the war and don't want to end up with their mothers crying over their graves. But this Johnny Reb's different. He's not starving, claims he never took part in any real fighting, and yet he deserts with a bizarre story that the war will end if we shoot General Lee in a place no one's even heard of before."

"So he's just another coward?"

"Maybe. On the other hand, if we decide the boy's story has merit, what do we do about it? If we try to kill Lee, how do we do it? Do we send one man to do the job? Do we send a company? A battalion? A regiment?" Pinckney sighed. "See what I mean?"

"Yeah, I doubt the army brass would risk one man or even a small detail to snuff out the life of one soldier. It just wouldn't make sound military sense."

"Right!" Pinckney clapped him on the shoulder. "By God, Bernie, I think you'll make an officer after all."

Woodside smiled in gratitude of the compliment, started to respond, but then thought better of it when the runner appeared.

His name was Willy Christiansen, a private of rank and the former regimental bugler who had turned seventeen just two weeks prior. The young man pulled himself together and saluted.

"Beg pardon, sir," he said, addressing Pinckney. He handed over a wrinkled sheet of paper.

Pinckney read what was on it, then a second time just to make sure. He heard Woodside say, "What is it, Colonel?"

"New orders." Pinckney gave it to him. "Take a look for yourself."

Woodside read.

"Well?" urged Pinckney.

"Don't know, Tom. All it says is that we're obliged to dispatch a reconnaissance patrol to look for a hole in the Reb lines. It doesn't give a reason why."

Pinckney said to Christiansen, "Where did this order come from?"

"Brigade headquarters, sir."

"Yes, I know that, Private, only who gave the order?"

"Some major I never seen before."

"Major!" Pinckney's face turned cherry red with anger. "I'm to take orders from a junior officer?"

"Must be a prank," suggested Woodside. To Christiansen he said, "You sure about this, Willy?"

"As God is my witness," answered the boy.

"What's this major's name?" Pinckney demanded of him.

"Well, Colonel, sir, let me think." Christiansen pressed his lips together, as though it would help him remember. At last he said, "His name is Steps." Then he corrected himself. "No, wait! It ain't Steps, it's Stairs. His name is Major Stairs."

Colonels in the Union army do not take orders from junior officers. However, for the first time in his military career, Colonel Thomas James Pinckney was compelled to do so when Joshua Stairs told him where the order had originated.

"General Grant gave the order?"

"That's right, Colonel."

"But I don't get it. What's it all about, Major?"

"The reason is unimportant. Your job, Colonel, is to send out a reconnaissance patrol to find a gap in the enemy lines." He unraveled a map and specified a particular spot. "I'm told your regiment is closest to the Reb pickets here."

"That's right," nodded Pinckney. "About three miles away."

"Perfect. When can you get started?"

"Anytime you say."

"Good, do it tonight, Colonel. I want that information no later than noon tomorrow."

Pinckney gnashed his teeth together, was an angry volcano ready to erupt. But he kept his composure and watched quietly as Stairs turned away without saluting and left.

Woodside waited until Stairs was out of earshot before he said to his boss, "How could you stand it, sir, taking orders from *that* man?"

Pinckney grabbed a pencil from the table and snapped it in

half.

"The bastard! Who the hell does he think he is? He wouldn't even tell me why he needed the information. I've a mind to—"

"Easy, Tom. Remember, he's General Grant's aide-de-camp. Don't go looking for trouble."

"I don't give a damn if he shines shoes for the president!"

Woodside suppressed a need to laugh, made a smirk instead, and said, "I wonder why he really needs that information."

"Who cares?"

"Hey, I got it, sir. Maybe he read your report about that Reb deserter we caught this morning. Maybe he thinks the boy's story about General Lee is true. If that's the case, maybe he wants to dispatch a cavalry detail to bushwhack him."

"Are you crazy, Lieutenant? That's the dumbest thing that's ever come out of your mouth. No, he just wants to give us something to do, that's all. Probably thinks we're bored."

"Guess you're right, Colonel. Still, you have to wonder what it's all about."

"It doesn't matter, orders are orders."

VII

Westmoreland and Stairs met again early on the afternoon of 27 October. The meeting was held in the duty hut of the Thirteenth Pennsylvania Regiment. Also in attendance was Sean O'Grady.

"There it is, Jon—the latest reconnaissance. Compliments of the Sixth New Hampshire Volunteers." Stairs pointed to the spot on the map he had circled with a pencil. It represented a bridge on the York River not far from enemy-held territory. "No activity here at all," he added.

"Hard to believe Johnny Reb wouldn't picket that bridge," said Westmoreland, shaking his head. "I don't like it, sir."

"Agreed, but it's your only way across the river. You see, the waterline is high due to the heavy rains the past few weeks. There's no suitable place to ford along that stretch of the river."

O'Grady interjected, "Beg pardon, Major."

"Yes, Sergeant?"

"Sir, all it would take is one Reb patrol to spot us and your plan is dog dirt. They get just one sharpshooter near that bridge and we ain't never gonna get across. Be like shootin' fish in a barrel."

Stairs ignored him.

"You'll need to leave early in the morning, preferably before dawn," Westmoreland heard him say. "This way you'll be across the river before dusk." He indicated another spot on the map. "Lee and his staff will be bivouacking here on the twenty-ninth. It will be your best chance to find him and make the kill."

Westmoreland's face clouded. He shot a glance at O'Grady, who was also wearing a bewildered mug. The former coal miner turned soldier opened his mouth to comment, but Stairs cut him off before he could utter a sound.

"Sergeant-Major, I need to speak to the captain in private now." He waved an impatient hand. "Dismissed."

O'Grady ground his teeth together, seeming as if poised to challenge the order, but was smart enough not to. He saluted like the obedient soldier he was, made an about-face and headed for the exit as fast as he could without being obvious about it. Westmoreland waited until he was out of hearing range before he told Stairs what he was thinking.

"I know what the sergeant wanted to say, Josh, so let me do it for him." He pointed to the spot on the map Stairs had indicated just moments earlier. "How do you know General Lee will be *here* on the twenty-ninth?"

"All right, Jon, suppose you have a right to know—but only you." Stairs took a deep breath and said when he exhaled, "We've got a spy at enemy headquarters."

Westmoreland's jaw dropped like a lead sinker through seawater.

"You're not serious?"

"No, it's true. We have an agent working in the heart of Lee's headquarters. 'Angel'—that's his cover name—has been feeding me information for the past several months. Tells me everything Lee is doing. His battle plans, where he is, where he's going, what he had for supper." A flippant smile by Grant's adjutant. "Things like that."

"Good God, Major!"

"Yes, hard to believe, isn't it? And that's why I chased the sergeant away. No one needs to know that information but you, Captain. In fact, General Grant and I are the only others who know about Angel."

"So we have a chance after all." Westmoreland had spoken as if addressing himself, as though Stairs were not there at all. "We really *do* have a chance to assassinate Lee."

"Yes, a very good chance."

"But if we succeed and don't return, no one will ever know."

"No, I hardly think that. Word of his death would

eventually leak out and end up in print. When the newspapers reach the public, anarchy will follow. The Confederacy will split apart and collapse—the whole rotten structure."

"You're sure about that, sir?"

"No," answered Stairs feebly, "of course I'm not."

His friend said, "If we succeed, Major, I'll do my best to make sure one of us returns with the news."

"No, not just anyone, Jon, you must be the one."

"Oh!" Westmoreland raised an inquisitive eyebrow. "Why is that?"

"Because you're an officer of credibility, a veteran soldier and holder of the Medal of Honor. Your word will be accepted as fact, and not a trumped-up story. When you return with confirmation of Lee's death, it will create a firestorm across the country, particularly in the south."

"And if I don't get back?"

"Just make sure you do. If not, the mission will have been an exercise in futility."

"You make it sound as if I can't come back unless Lee is killed."

"Sorry, Jon, didn't mean to give you that impression. But this is no ordinary job, perhaps the toughest you've ever had to do. Believe me, I don't envy the task awaiting you. However, I do envy your inevitable success."

They shook hands.

Stairs said, "I'll be leaving for City Point in the morning. Before I go, there's one more thing I'd like you to do for me."

"Sir?"

"Come on—you'll see."

*   *   *

Ulysses S. Grant yanked the cigar from his mouth and reached for the bottle of whiskey on the map table. As he poured, he acknowledged the young man seated opposite him with a grin.

"Sure you wouldn't like a dram, Captain?"

"No, thank you, sir."

Grant sipped, swallowed and said, "I'll never forget how long it took us to capture Vicksburg last year. Pemberton's army put up one helluva fight. Most of all, I'll never forget the daily casualty reports. After a while I couldn't look at them."

"I know what you mean, sir."

Grant continued, "At first I was reluctant to approve the major's plan. Let's face it, General Lee is no ordinary soldier. For me, a former comrade-in-arms. But now he's the enemy, wears a different uniform.

"Yes, Lee is the reason the Confederacy has lasted as long as it has. In fact, some of my staff officers refer to him as the devil in human form." Grant punctuated his words with an insincere chuckle.

Stairs said, "Believe it was I who first said that, General."

Grant nodded indifferently, drank some more, and said to the Pennsylvania cavalryman, "Major Stairs and I are of the opinion that if anyone can succeed in eliminating Lee, it is you, Captain. You have an outstanding record of achievement, not to mention the respect and loyalty of your men. It is a combination of that loyalty and respect which makes for an outstanding officer."

"I'll do my best," Jon told him.

Grant carried on, "I don't like giving the order to assassinate Lee. In fact, it may be the most difficult decision I've ever had to make in my military career. However, it must be done. The president wants this godforsaken war to end now." The great man stood, waited for Westmoreland to do the same, and held out his hand. "Good luck, Captain." They shook hands. "Godspeed!"

Stairs said, "Best of luck, Jon." He stepped closer, offered his hand, and Westmoreland seized it with affection.

"Thanks, Josh."

No more talk was necessary. Westmoreland faced Grant, snapped his heels together and saluted. Grant reciprocated, and he and Stairs watched as Westmoreland turned away and left the railway car.

Stairs sauntered over to the window and peered out, watching as his friend disappeared behind a wall of boxcars, wondering if he had just seen him for the last time. When he turned back, he found the general refilling his tumbler.

"A dirty business, Major," Grant said to the glass.

"Sir, you've had reservations about this mission from the beginning. You don't believe it'll work, despite the planning."

"My honest opinion, it would take a miracle," was Grant's reply. "For instance, it all depends on precise timing and whether or not Lee is where he's supposed to be on the day after tomorrow. How can you be sure the information we've received is accurate?"

"I regret to say, I can't guarantee anything, sir. We can only hope it's accurate."

"This spy at Lee's headquarters. What was his name

again?"

"We don't know his true identity, General. We only know him by his cover name, 'Angel'."

Grant poured.

"Too bad the spy can't kill Lee for us," he said thoughtfully.

"Yes, sir, but that's impossible. And I think you know why."

"Yes, that I do remember, Major." Grant shook his head sadly. "A terrible shame, that."

The woods were crowded with soldiers. Sharpshooters, the lucky ones who had survived, were dug in seemingly behind every rock and tree. Scattered around them were the dead. The others, the wounded, would not last long in the stifling heat of the afternoon.

The Confederate prize, the small mountain in their way, would never be claimed that day. A strange, funny name it had too. The locals called it Little Round Top. The Union defense, although suspect on paper, would bend but not break on that fateful second day in July of '63. The defenders proudly called themselves the 16th Michigan, the 44th New York, the 83rd Pennsylvania, and the 20th Maine. When the battle was over, they became immortal.

Jon Westmoreland's brother, Peter, became immortal that day. Abraham Lincoln made sure of it four months later when he traveled to Gettysburg and dedicated the Federal cemetery to those who had fallen in his "Fourscore and seven years ago" address to the nation. Peter Westmoreland, a patriotic, twenty-seven-year-old volunteer who'd had aspirations of becoming a trial lawyer after the war, had taken cannon shrapnel in both lungs and died instantly in the presence of his comrades, who wept later as they buried him not far from where he had fallen. Jon Westmoreland wept on the day he received the letter informing him of his big brother's death. It happened nearly three weeks after the great battle had ended.

He remembered that time as if it were yesterday. He wished he had been at Gettysburg serving in General George Armstrong Custer's elite cavalry. Instead, he was doing his duty in Mississippi as Vicksburg fell to Ulysses S. Grant.

He collected his thoughts and inspected the five soldiers standing in line in front of him, the same who had volunteered to serve with him on a secret mission that would "end the war" and reunite a blood-stained country torn apart by political ideology. Five young men he had grown to admire who believed in a cause for which thousands had fought and died. They were Pennsylvania born and bred, except for one, but all were Americans—*his* men. Would they end up like the rest, the fallen of Manassas, Antietam, Fredericksburg, and the countless other battles?

Westmoreland looked them over again, slowly, one by one. At the end of the line on his right was Private Andrew "Shorty" Jones, the youngest and smallest of the group. Jones was a quiet, introverted young man who never seemed bothered by anything, including the thought of dying for his country: an obedient young man who answered orders with a firm salute and no debate.

Next to Jones was Jake Carson. The corporal was two

years younger than O'Grady, the eldest: an expert horseman who had ridden more than twenty miles one rainy afternoon with a bullet lodged in his right thigh and didn't realize it until he climbed down from the saddle. Carson still had the scar and perpetual limp to prove to the world it had really happened.

On Carson's right was the unflappable and popular Ohioan, William Flanagan. The lanky corporal was O'Grady's best friend: a twenty-three-year-old who loved to have fun the moment the opportunity presented itself. He was also a dedicated, trustworthy sort who was dead serious about his soldiering. Yes, a good man to have around, especially when things got rough. Billy would keep the others loose and ready for the unexpected.

Corporal Zachary Miller stood next to him. Miller was a veteran of three major campaigns who liked to pull a cork more often than not: a born troublemaker, and yet one who could shoot a carbine rifle better than anyone he knew. Like the others, Miller was an asset to the group despite his established shortcomings. No doubt about that.

Westmoreland turned to O'Grady, the last in line, and smiled. The man was a rock, the glue that held the others together and working as a team. Issuing orders was easy with the sergeant-major at his side. For this mission, he would need him more than ever if indeed they hoped to succeed, and survive.

"We'll leave before sunrise," he told them. "By noon we'll be deep in enemy territory."

Silence.

He said to O'Grady, "You've issued the proper amount of rations and cartridges?"

"Yes, sir, enough for three days."

"Very well." A moment of hesitation, a large gulp of air before he continued, "I'm not going to repeat myself by telling you what this mission means, nor am I going to waste your time by reminding you of your duty. I wish I could promise you that we'll all make it back alive, but I can't. However, I do know that I couldn't have picked a better detail for this assignment. I just hope I don't let you down."

Flanagan said, "Beg pardon, Cap'n, but that's the first time I ever heared you talk crap."

"Billy's right," joined in O'Grady. "You ain't never let us down. For my money, you're the best officer in the army. If I could choose a way to die in this war, it would be with you and the boys."

"That's a fact," added Miller.

Smiling, Westmoreland dismissed them before they could see the moisture welling up in his eyes. For the next hour he studied the map, memorizing the route they would take and creating in his mind the right conclusion to the job awaiting them.

He spied the letter he had written the night before. It was on the table next to the bed, sealed in an envelope and ready for the morning mail pickup. It was a short letter, direct and to the point, unlike the others he had written to her. He sat down on the bed, grabbed the envelope and sighed, its contents still fresh in his mind...

Dear Alice,

I regret to say that this will be my last letter for a while. Tomorrow I leave on special assignment. I'm not sure how long it will take, but I'm certain it will be several days before I can take pencil in hand again.

I want you to remember that I'll always love you, no matter what happens to me. You've given me much happiness in the short time we've been married. God willing, I'll return to you one day and we shall resume our lives as husband and wife.

Please believe me when I say that what I'm doing is important to the war effort. If I don't return, trust in God that it was His will, and that I shall miss you until we meet again in His everlasting glory.

Love, Jon

VIII

The river current seemed calm enough, virtually little movement visible to the naked eye. Thick layers of red mud lined both banks of the York, a consequence of the torrential rains of the past fortnight. Ice, the product of an overnight chill, had formed along the river's apron but soon vanished after the start of dawn. It was a sober reminder that winter was just around the corner, waiting to strike.

The winter of 1864 would be a harsh one. Elderly Virginians would remember it as one of the worst of the century. Autumn would also be remembered as one of the worst. Some would say it was the war which added the extra chill to the air, more bite to the wind that always seemed to originate from the north.

The cavalrymen had ridden all morning of the twenty-eighth under foreboding clouds of steel gray, making good time and without incident. It was early in the afternoon when they reached their first objective.

The bridge, history tells, had been constructed from native lumber and by the skilled hands of free labor—African slaves. Although its better days had come and gone, the bridge was structurally sound despite its obvious dilapidated appearance. To safely cross over the soldiers would need to proceed on foot, one by one, for the bridge was quite narrow, had just enough room for rider and horse. On the opposite side tall trees of maple and elm crowded the shoreline. The perfect redoubt for enemy snipers to do their dirty work.

"Don't like it, Cap'n." It was O'Grady's whisper behind him. "Ain't nothin' here but trouble. Let's find another way across."

Westmoreland removed the field glasses from his eyes.

"No, Sergeant, there's no suitable ford along this stretch of the river. We've no choice but to cross here."

"But, sir, can't it wait till dark? The Rebs might have a brigade of sharpshooters behind them trees and pick us off one by one. At least in the dark we'd stand a fair chance of making it across."

"No, we can't wait. We must stick to our timetable. If we don't, we'll never complete our objective."

"But it's too risky, Jon!"

Ignoring him, Westmoreland reached inside his saddlebag

and yanked out a silver pocket watch, a gift from his parents on his seventeenth birthday, the day he had learned of his appointment to the military academy at West Point. He opened the cover and noted the time.

"All right, let's get started," he said, his words for O'Grady. "I'll be first to go. Wait till I'm across, then you and the others follow in turn. But wait for my signal. If it's a trap, turn back and head for home. That's an order."

"But, sir, if they got snipers in them trees and shoot you down, we just can't leave you there to rot."

"Don't argue with me, Sergeant. Now let's get cracking!"

Westmoreland dismounted and started across the bridge, reins in hand. Not much later he was standing on the enemy side of the river, his face fastened to a broad, triumphant grin. He shoved his left hand high over his head and waved. O'Grady acknowledged the signal with a similar gesture and turned, facing Miller.

"Okay, Zack, you're next, off you go."

Miller hitched up his pants and did as he was told. When he joined Westmoreland at the other side, they saw a smiling Shorty Jones moving toward them at a brisk pace. Next to cross over was Flanagan, followed in step by the limping Carson. O'Grady remained where he was. Westmoreland waved.

O'Grady closed his eyes, mumbled the only biblical words he knew, reopened them and started across the bridge at turtle-like speed, unaware he had stopped breathing in the usual fashion. He arrived on the other side of the river gulping huge portions of air much faster than he needed to.

Westmoreland frowned, not liking what he saw.

"You all right, Sean?"

O'Grady bobbed his head, proving he was, although the color on his face showed a different story.

"You're whiter than a cloud, Sergeant," spouted a grinning Miller. "What happened, you get sea sick?"

"No, I…can't swim," O'Grady said to his boots, provoking a chorus of laughter from the others. He looked up, embarrassed. "Don't worry, Cap'n, I'm okay."

Westmoreland said to Carson, "You and Shorty scout ahead and see what you can find. Report back in fifteen minutes."

The two soldiers mounted and left the bridge at the half gallop. They returned twenty minutes later according to Westmoreland's pocket watch. Jake Carson, the elder of the two and higher in rank, provided Westmoreland with a detailed account of what they had seen, which included a brief encounter with a family of deer. There were no signs of enemy patrols, he added. Satisfied, Westmoreland produced a map from his saddlebag and verified their position.

"From here we head south, then due west when we reach the main road," he told them. To O'Grady he said, "Take the point, Sergeant-Major. If we're lucky, we'll be exactly where we're supposed to be in twenty-four hours."

They rode hard and fast the first hour after leaving the bridge before settling into a cavalryman's trot for the benefit of the animals. Rain happened around noon, although it lasted barely long enough to be remembered. When they reached the east-west turnpike, Westmoreland ordered a halt. The plan from here on, he told them, would be to follow the road at a parallel course. "It should keep us from being spotted by enemy patrols."

The first sign of trouble occurred later in the afternoon. Billy Flanagan, who had been sent ahead to scout a small tobacco farm, encountered two Negro boys fishing by a narrow stream, not far from what looked to be an old curing shed. The Ohioan managed to remain out of sight of the pair, watching them with a grin as they went about their business. Several minutes later a white-haired black man with a tired stride arrived at the fishing spot. The man, who seemed old enough to be the grandparent of the two, seized the youngsters by their ears and led them away from the stream, lecturing them along the way of the consequences of not completing their chores on time. It was an hour before dusk during another cloudburst when the ambush took place.

The rapid volley of gunfire seemed to come from every direction. Jake Carson, riding point, was stopped by a flurry of buckshot and died seconds later still attached to the saddle. Westmoreland had no time to watch it happen when his horse staggered under him. The rifle bullets, which had pierced the gelding's neck, were enough to bring the black horse crashing to the ground. Thrown from the saddle, Westmoreland hit the ground hard, badly bruised and barely alive. The others, riding in single file behind him, were not as fortunate.

Like Carson, Shorty Jones was already dead from his three chest wounds, and Billy Flanagan was dying where he had fallen, buried under his crippled mare, hands still clutching the reins. Amazingly enough, Sean O'Grady survived the initial hailstorm of enemy bullets, but not the second. Zack Miller, riding drag, saw his friend collapse in the saddle after the mini ball struck him flush in the Adam's apple, then die from a second gunshot wound which sent him tumbling to the earth. Left arm bleeding from a prior wound, Miller managed to grab hold of his rifle and shout a barrage of expletives at his foe, but was unable to get a shot off when the final round heard that day exploded in his chest, making a wide hole in his heart. He was dead before he hit the ground.

The lone survivor of the attack, Westmoreland lay unconscious in a nest of wet underbrush. Like his comrades, he would never meet the soldiers responsible for bushwhacking his team. The foot patrol of Confederate sharpshooters, commanded by a North Carolinian named Marsh, a captain of rank who in a hearing after the war defended his action that day as "my soldierly duty," remained at the scene only to corral the two surviving horses. "T'was no sense in leaving 'em behind," he told his superior when he made his report the next day. Behind them the ambushers left four animals dead and rotting, five enemy horse soldiers killed, and another not knowing whether he would live or not. It was five minutes after the rebels had fled when the rain stopped and the sun reappeared in a gorgeous blue sky.

Robert E. Lee removed his spectacles and looked up from the map. For a long moment he stared at Taylor, who was standing patiently at the opposite side of the map table. He cleared his throat.

"I don't like the idea of leaving the army at this time," he said, using a somber tone. "However, I suppose this trip to Richmond will serve its purpose."

"Sir, I wish you'd reconsider. As I mentioned this morning, we've received several reports of enemy reconnaissance the past two days. Maybe you should postpone the trip until we discover what they're up to. It's possible Grant is preparing for an offensive."

"I shall take your opinion under advisement, Colonel. However, I sincerely doubt he'll attack at this time, especially after all the rain we've had. Besides, I don't want to postpone this trip any longer than I have to. It's too important."

"But, General, think of the consequences if something happens to you. The army will be without your leadership, sir. The country cannot afford to lose you."

"No, Colonel, I will not postpone this trip. It's the best way I know to petition the president for the food and weapons we need."

"But, sir, do you truly believe he'll agree to your demands?"

"Hard to say, Colonel. The south has very little to offer now, particularly in the way of men and provisions."

The words came out of his mouth softly, without the usual pitch of confidence. Most unbecoming of the great man.

"General, forgive me for saying so, but is the war lost? Is there no chance of victory anymore?"

Lee hesitated. How would he reply? Although the answer seemed obvious, the thought of defeat left an ugly scar in his mind, especially after so many had given the ultimate sacrifice.

"Colonel," he said, "the matter has always been in the hands of Almighty God. We've done our duty and must continue to do so until He decides otherwise."

The answer put a sparkle in Taylor's eyes.

"General, I truly believe that no one fully understands the burden you carry on your shoulders each day the war goes on. I can think of no one I admire more than you, sir." He stiffened. "Now if you'll please excuse me?" Lee gave his consent with a nod, Taylor saluted and headed for the exit.

When he was gone, Lee glanced down at the map. After a while his mind started to wander. Yes, the war was in the hands of Almighty God, and yet he alone would be held accountable for the actions of the Army of Northern Virginia. Still, did the South ever have a chance against a foe of seemingly inexhaustible men and steel? No, probably not. That man in Washington was adamant and would never quit until surrender of the Confederacy was absolute. Lee turned away from the map table, massaging his aching forehead. Yes, that man in Washington was adamant, and yet one had to respect him, for he, too, knew the war was in the hands of the Almighty.

Later that day as the sun slipped behind a new curtain of storm clouds, Jon Westmoreland stirred and came awake. He squinted at his new surroundings and tried to focus as he raised his head. But the strain was too much, and he slumped back down into the moist underbrush, closed his eyes and slept.

IX

He had slept for several hours—or had it been only for a few minutes? Just how long was impossible to know.

At that moment time seemed at a standstill, had no meaning for him. As the eyelids came apart, he was aware of a feeling of emptiness, of loneliness. His vision was fuzzy, and his head throbbed at will. When his sight cleared, the first thing he saw was the red maple standing over him, beads of rain water dripping from its sagging, naked branches. There was something in the wind too, a distinct, foul odor that was familiar to him, for he had experienced the scent many times before. Only he couldn't remember where or when.

That which had aroused his sense of smell was the stench of dead horse flesh: the black stallion lying just several yards from him. The picture of the dead animal blurred suddenly, he blinked, again, and his tired eyes came back into focus. He saw three other horses lying on the ground not far away, each in the same position as the one nearest him. He wondered what had happened to them, why he did not know the answer.

He sat up and spotted the human bodies scattered nearby: men in blue military uniforms, just like the type he was wearing. The pounding inside his skull was unyielding as he stood and counted the inert bodies. Two...four...five in all. He stepped toward the largest of the five, the one with the gray-flecked dark hair and beard. Darned on each of his sleeves were three, V-shaped white stripes stacked vertically, distinguishing him as a soldier of experience and responsibility. There was no breathing, he saw, nor movement of any kind. Strange, but something inside him told him that he knew this man. Only who was he? What was his name?

He studied the other corpses, one by one. They were all young men, their faces calm and ghostly pale, each wearing at least one marble-sized gunshot wound in his rain-drenched uniform. They had bled to death, that much was obvious, though the evidence of blood was gone, had been washed away by the rain. He knew these men too, of that he was certain. Yet what were their names? Why did he not know them?

He walked away from the remains of Billy Flanagan and

sat under an old, weary-looking elm tree. What had happened here? Had there been some kind of skirmish? If so, why had he not perished along with the others? He reached up and rubbed his forehead with care. The pain inside was merciless.

He glanced around and counted again. Five soldiers—all dead. But why? What was the reason? He tried to think, to remember, only it didn't work. Yet something told him that he belonged with these men, knew who they were. The sun punched a hole in the treetops, pinpointing his face, and he squinted and turned away. Then, as suddenly as it had appeared, the sunlight vanished. He stood carefully and looked around. Where was he?

Dear God, help me!

He inhaled for strength and started to walk, unsure where he was heading or what he would do once he got there. After a while he stopped, glanced over his shoulder and tried once again to recall what had happened to the others and why his life had been spared, had no meaning. Was he in some way responsible for the terrible incident which had occurred there? He grimaced as he reached up again and massaged the throbbing forehead. No, none of it made sense. Why could he not remember?

He felt drowsy suddenly, the legs heavier, unable to go on. He sat down under a dogwood tree and closed his eyes.

The pain! Oh, God, the pain!

Jonathan Westmoreland lay down on the wet grass, rolled over on his side and fell asleep. Then it started to drizzle.

The tall ship which ferried M'bida from western Africa to the

British colonies in North America was the *King George*. Sold by black slave owners to white slave traders in the southernmost port of what would become Côte d'Ivoire in the twentieth century, M'bida had just turned thirteen when she embarked on the sea voyage to the New World.

Accompanying her were more than three hundred other blacks destined to live out their lives in bondage, many having not yet reached puberty. Tragically, nearly ten percent of the slaves perished in the damp, overcrowded holds beneath the decks. Some died of malnutrition, while others from various diseases or self-inflicted wounds. Some even committed suicide or were murdered out of hand. The majority of slaves who did survive would later wish they had not.

The *King George* arrived in America in September 1768 in a place the English called Hatteras Island. First things first, she was auctioned off to the highest bidder. To her surprise, she was treated with respect by the tall white man from Virginia who had purchased her. She was fed well, given clean clothes to replace the rags she had worn during the sea crossing, and slept under a dry roof with the others whom she would later claim as her family. None of it made sense, of course, for she had expected quite the opposite from her new master.

The first few years were the most difficult for her. She was obliged to accept her new surname, Madden, and learn the strange customs of the English. Of all, it was the language lessons she despised, although it had nothing to do with her ability to comprehend. She was unusually bright compared to most slaves her age, could perform any chore given to her by her English matron. Her main function in life, she was told, was to indulge in the breeding of muscular young men who would till and harvest the great fields of corn, tobacco and cotton. It was a duty she would perform with dedication.

By the time she turned twenty-three, M'bida had given birth to five children, four of them males, of whom two had died at the time of delivery. The surviving trio lived out their lives laboring in the sweltering fields, horse barns and curing sheds. By the age of thirty-four her breeding days were over, but not before she had delivered six more field hands to follow in the footsteps of their elder siblings.

By then the Madden property had become a prosperous thousand-acre plantation. Which was amazing, considering it had happened during what the colonials called the war for independence. After the great conflict was settled in favor of the Americans, their former landlords abdicated and a new government was formed in its stead. The fledgling nation baptized itself the United States of America and declared itself a democracy, with "life, liberty and the pursuit of happiness" for all. That is, except for the Negro.

With the birth of the thirteen-state republic and the dawn of a new century spawned much hope and prosperity for many. Everywhere was a bounty of frontier adventure awaiting those who dared. The south, rich with oceans of land for plow and seed, prospered like never before. Unlike the more industrialized northern states, the south employed a traditional, if not medieval agricultural system that was managed by the whip and lubricated by the blood, sweat and tears of the Africans.

Still, existing as a slave in the new land of freedom and

opportunity was a far better life for most Negroes who had experienced far worse in their tribal homelands. Although the work was demanding of them, the blacks flourished as a race. Land barons, mindful that their bread was buttered at the expense of the slaves, provided them with warm clothing, solid living huts and acres of food for the dinner table, thus ensuring the livelihoods of future generations. It seemed the perfect system.

But as the country grew, so did a society of men who demanded of the government that a redefinition of liberty was long overdue. Freedom for all must include the Negro too, they proclaimed. They called themselves abolitionists and spread their ideas, radical to some, from one state to the next. States that enacted laws to abolish slavery were those of the north, while the majority of southern states remained adamant in their ways. They were immune, they declared, their sovereign right to conduct business the way they saw fit protected by the sacred words of the Constitution. Before long, the battle line was drawn in Congress between North and South. For those Americans who could think past their next meal, war was inevitable.

The second revolution to decide the fate of the republic began in Charleston Harbor on 12 April 1861 as Confederate mortars under the command of Brigadier General Pierre G. T. Beauregard opened fire on the Federal garrison at Fort Sumter. Two days later the Union flag was hauled down by the victorious South Carolinians. It would take four long years and more than a half million dead before the Stars and Stripes was unfurled over the harbor again by General Robert

Anderson, the man whom Beauregard had defeated.

M'bida died of pneumonia twenty years before the winter of the first year of the War Between the States. She was survived by three offspring, fourteen grandchildren, and eighty-one of her grandchildren's children. Despite escalating privations in Virginia and most other southern states, the Madden plantation flourished, providing much needed food, tobacco and horse fodder for Jefferson Davis' gray army: an army of invincibility during the early stages of the conflict. Only it wouldn't last. When Southern forces at Vicksburg fell to Ulysses S. Grant on 1 July '63, followed by Lee's defeat at Gettysburg two days later, the Confederacy was doomed. Final defeat was just a matter of when.

As the Army of Northern Virginia limped across the Potomac following the Gettysburg debacle, rumors of impending defeat spread throughout the South, destroying the morale of the citizenry. The majority of slaves, having been awarded their freedom by President Lincoln, seized the opportunity and bolted, their destination anywhere north of the Mason-Dixon Line. Their method of travel, a risky, painstaking ordeal, was by way of the Underground Railroad. However, many slaves did not survive the journey to reap the benefits they had so long awaited.

The Madden property was not immune to the mass exodus of freedom-seekers. Of the two hundred Madden slaves, just twenty-one stayed behind, the majority due to old age or failing health. Others remained simply because they were apprehensive of an unknown future up north. Eventually all but two of the slaves fled the plantation. One was M'bida's grandson, who was terminally ill with tuberculosis. The other was his only daughter. Her African name was Ekeke, although she was better known by her adopted one, Elsie.

Elsie Madden would be fifteen years old on the day after the Christmas of 1864. She was small and wiry, had seldom worked as a laborer in the fields. Her main duty was to cook and care for the Madden household. Like her great-grandmother, Elsie surprised people with her quick learning ability, absorbing knowledge like a sponge. She was particularly fond of the teachings of the Bible and had made God her constant companion. "He will see me through the bad times" was her favorite phrase when she was depressed or lonely.

The sun was already high in the morning sky as Elsie stepped out of the henhouse carrying a pail of ground Indian corn. Cradled in her other hand were three eggs she would eat for breakfast. A quarter mile away was the Madden mansion, its sturdy pillars no longer white but dirty gray, the picket fence standing guard around it in disrepair. Without its residents, the great house of nineteen rooms was a hollow shell. The owner of the estate, her master, James Everett Madden III, descendent of the man who had purchased her great-grandmother at auction a century earlier, had left for military service and never returned. Had it not been for her father, whom she had watched die and buried the month before, Elsie would have left with the others.

She started away from the henhouse, heading toward the wide meadow directly in her path. The land had been cleared for the graves of deceased slaves who had worked for the Madden dynasty. Her great-grandmother was there, along with several of her offspring. Now her father rested there for eternity. She stopped when she saw his grave, the one she had carved out of the earth with her own hands. The wooden cross at the head of the grave had shifted to one side, so she reached down and straightened it, knowing that someday she would rest there beside him.

She left the meadow and made breakfast. Afterwards she chopped up some wood for the fireplace, the same that would keep her warm during the night ahead. At noon she fed the chickens, then decided to head for the stream and try her luck with her fishing stick. The heavy rains of the past fortnight had softened the earth, allowing for plenty of worms to be harvested as bait. The day was still bright and pleasantly warm as she headed northwest into the woods, thinking of the speckled trout she would land for dinner.

The Lord is my shepherd; I shall not want...

She recited her father's favorite psalm in her mind, giving her something to do as she followed the muddy path toward the stream. Squirrels were out in abundance, foraging in preparation of the winter months ahead. When she arrived at the brook, she felt the smile blossom on her lips. The water was calm and crystal clear, inviting her in. Perhaps she would take a bath today.

She walked to the edge of the stream with her smile still intact and tested the water with her bare feet. Cool, it was, but not too cold to bathe. As she started to strip down, she spotted the prostrate body lying under the dogwood tree not more than fifteen yards away. The body was that of a man in blue clothes.

A soldier of Mista Linkum's army?

She had never seen a blue-clad soldier before, only the ones in gray and butternut brown. She stepped closer when she noticed the breathing and slowly knelt beside him. He was a trim, handsome man who wore a thin shadow of facial hair. The hair on his crown, plastered to the scalp by the morning rain, was as black as the skin on her body. He was asleep, with legs curled up in the fetal position of a newborn, hands clutching his shoulders. He was shivering.

Elsie reached closer and touched his forehead. It felt warm, moist with perspiration. She dropped her chin and closed her eyes.

Thou shalt love thy neighbor!

She vaulted to her feet and raced home, knowing what had to be done. When she returned to the brook with blankets in hand, the soldier was exactly where she had found him. She hesitated, but then knelt beside him and went to work.

X

Light in the shanty was dull, yet sufficient enough to serve its purpose. Most was provided by a crackling log fire in the cooking hearth at the side of the room opposite the front door. The rest came from a lone candle standing tall on a small table not far from the bed, its pointed glow adding a halo effect to the wooden ceiling above him. Behind the table was a Bible sitting alone atop a rocking chair, the gray cover holding it together worn down from four generations of use.

Jonathan Westmoreland closed his eyes, reopened them and saw the exact same thing. Not long ago he had been lying in a meadow near a wooded stream, trembling at will, his clothes damp with rain. He saw the mounds of dead horses pop into his mind, four in all, along with the inert remains of five blue-clad soldiers whom he recognized, but whose names were still a mystery. Who were they? Who was he?

Attention! Your name, soldier! What is your name?

He reached up and gently touched his brow. The skin was warm, clammy with sweat, and he remembered the throbbing pain that had been there earlier. It was then he spotted his uniform hanging from a stud in the wall next to the fireplace. Someone had stripped him of it and placed it there, that much was certain. Yet he *was* wearing something. Slowly, he peeled the blankets aside and found himself attached to a different uniform, a gray one, complete with two vertical lines of brass buttons holding the blouse together, white stripes along the trouser legs, and an odd-shaped pattern of yellow curlicues wearing on the forearms of both sleeves.

Westmoreland shut his eyes and tried to remember. Blue and gray. Blue soldiers versus gray soldiers. He was a participant in a great war between the blue army and the gray army. He was a soldier of the blue army, yes, but his uniform had been removed and he was now wearing one of gray, the garb of his enemy. He raised his head and sat up, but the strain was too much and he flopped back down on the pillow. The Bible on the rocking chair captured his interest, and he sighed. Where was he? What was he going to do about it?

Oh, God, help me remember!

He slept for almost two hours and awoke when the black girl appeared in the shanty, a load of firewood cradled in her arms. She stopped when she saw him, but made no attempt to communicate. He watched as she stacked the wood against the wall next to the hearth, dropped a piece on the fire and waited until it flared. When she turned around, she found him staring at her with eyes wide and alert, full of questions.

Westmoreland made another attempt to sit up, but again the strain was too much and he fell back down on the bed, both eyes disappearing on impact. When he reopened them, she was standing next to the bed, staring down at him. She owned a serene-like oval face lacking of skin texture, and her physique was skeletal thin, giving him the impression that she had not eaten a proper meal in a week or so, perhaps longer.

"You all right, mista soldier?"

Her words were sturdy but gentle in tone, reminding him of another female's voice. Only who was she? What did she look like?

"You must rest some more," she said. She reached down and raised the blankets up to his chin. "You need to stay warm, sir. You was with fever not long ago." She stepped back across the room, grabbed another piece of wood and added it to the fire. "Might come back if you don't take care."

"Who are you?" he urged.

His question startled her. She spun around and was surprised to find him sitting up in the bed, back propped against the wall. For a long moment nothing happened between them. Then, as if remembering what to do, she stepped away from the hearth with more purpose in her stride and stood next to the bed. She wanted to reach closer, but she hesitated, stopping herself from touching him.

"Mista soldier, you *must* rest. Please, in God's name!"

He lay down, mainly because it was more painful not to, and looked her over. The pale blue cotton dress she wore seemed new. Tied at her waist was a soiled white apron showing much evidence of wear and tear. Hanging from her shoulders was a woolen shawl of red crotchet, telling him that it was cool outside. A frail-looking person, she had to be no more than fifteen years old, he estimated. Although he had seen many Negroes before, he could not recall where or when. He smiled at her, remembering she had called him "mista soldier".

Attention! Your name, soldier! What is your name?

"You didn't answer my question," he said abruptly. "What is your name, girl?"

"Elsie, sir, Elsie Madden."

"You live here?"

"Yes, sir."

"Alone?"

"Yes, sir. They's all gone."

"Who? Who are 'they'?"

"Why, the others, sir." She stared at him with squinting eyes, surprised by the mask of confusion he wore. "Don't you know, sir? I is a slave. Been workin' on this here farm since I be a girl."

"Farm?"

"Yes, sir. This place is the home of my daddy…and his daddy a'fore him."

"You said the others are gone. What others?"

"Why, the black peoples—like me."

"Where did they go?"

"Don't know for sure, but somewhere up north, I reckon. They left 'cause Mista Linkum told us we was free. But not all left, mind you. Some stayed behind with the old and the sick, like my daddy. Then Corn'l Madden left."

"Who's Colonel Madden?"

"Why, Corn'l Madden is Corn'l Madden. He owns this here farm. They say he was kilt in a great battle near Richmond city last spring. When his family went away, the black peoples went away too. You see, there's nobody here but me and my daddy." She looked away suddenly and dropped her chin, her sad eyes sparkling with moisture. "But he died 'bout a month a'fore. Buried him, I did."

"This uniform I'm wearing, did it belong to Colonel Madden?"

"Yes, sir." She indicated his uniform hanging from the wall near the fireplace. "Your clothes was wet. Took 'em off, you see, or you be sick with fever."

"I'm grateful for what you did, Elsie." Again the eyes flickered, then disappeared altogether.

He heard her say, "You all right, mista soldier?"

His eyes returned and he stared at her, surprised by the tone of concern she had used. He was still bemused as to why the skinny black girl had gone to the trouble of helping him in his moment of need. She was so polite and kind to him, yet there was something else. She was intelligent, despite the horrible grammar, and seemed plenty mature for her age.

He said, "I feel light-headed...and thirsty."

"I'll fetch some water," she told him.

When she returned later with a pail of cold well water, he was asleep. She watched him for a while, wondering if he would ever recover. She stepped across the room and reached for a piece of firewood.

She sat in her father's rocking chair by the fireplace, the Bible open across her lap, and prayed for him during the night. His fever had returned, was worse than before, and he tossed and turned a lot, moaning and grumbling in his sleep. At times he mumbled the names of places foreign to her. He called them West Point, Pittsburg Landing, Vicksburg, Cold Harbor. At other times he recited the names of people. One he repeated several times was Peter, who was, she presumed, a close comrade or relative. She knew that by the tone of reverence in his voice. He also muttered "Alice" over and over, a name he referenced with much affection during his calmer moments. She wondered if Alice was his mother, or sister, or sweetheart. Or was she his wife?

His fever broke just after dawn the following day. She gave him water to drink, but he was still not strong enough to eat and drifted back to sleep. A half hour passed before he woke up and saw that she had gone. It was warm in the shanty despite the fact the fire in the hearth had burned itself out, and sunlight streamed into the room through a small hole in the window curtain directly behind the bed.

Elsie returned to the shanty later and was surprised to find him awake. She was wearing old gloves and a dark woolen shirt tucked inside a pair of baggy denim trousers: clothes that seemed better suited for a man. The shoes she wore, which were caked with mud, appeared to be the only things that fit her properly. Covering her hair like a crown was a faded green kerchief in the shape of a turban. She removed the gloves, stepped closer and touched his forehead with the back of her hand.

"Praise the Lord!" she said. "Your fever went away. How you feel, mista soldier?"

"Tired—very tired," he said. "I feel like I've been asleep forever. But I think I'll live." He smiled at her. "I owe you my thanks."

"No, t'was not me a'tall, it was *Him*." She glanced up at the ceiling for effect. "The Lord said you would live, sir."

"Where am I? Is this your home?"

"Yes, sir. I been livin' here a long time."

"Where is 'here'? What is this place called?"

"Why, this here farm belong to Corn'l Madden—Corn'l James Madden."

"Yes, you've already told me that. But what town is nearby? Do you know where this place is on the map?"

"Don't reckon I never seen a map a'fore. All I know, this farm is 'bout a half day ride from Willistown. That's east, you know. Ever heared of it?"

"No," he said. Then she changed the subject.

"Why is you here, mista soldier?"

"I don't know," he answered, speaking to the ceiling.

"Did you ran away from the army?" was her next question.

"I don't know what happened to me. I seem to have forgotten."

"You is the first Yankee soldier I ever seen," she said. "My daddy said he seen many Yankees, but that was a'fore the war. Masta Jim let many white peoples come to the farm, mostly in summertime. Many come from Mary-land. I 'member 'cause I made lemon tea and party cakes for the white peoples when they was hungry. Played games with all the white kids."

"Why didn't you leave with the other coloreds?" he asked, switching topics. "Why did you stay here?"

"'Cause I could never leave my daddy, he was too sick and feeble." She stared across the room at nothing in particular. "My daddy was everything to me. Did never want to leave him."

"Is there anything to eat?"

She prepared a bowl of grits for him to go along with a small slice of smoked ham she had fetched from the curing shed. Although he enjoyed the taste of the meat, he was unable to keep most of it down. Fortunately the dandelion tea she gave him helped to settle his stomach. Afterwards he felt relaxed, but was still not strong enough to stand on his feet. But he was not sleepy, and they continued in conversation.

"I never knew a slave before," he told her. "Tell me about your father. What did he do here?"

"He was Masta Jim's groom. He loved horses, my daddy did. Liked 'em better than peoples sometime. I 'member him sayin', 'When you sit tall on a horse, you stand close to God.'" She punctuated her words with a proud smile.

"You told me that your father died about a month ago, and yet you stayed here. Aren't you lonely?"

"No, sir, I got the Lord to keep me company. He looks after me."

"But you can't stay here forever."

"But where do I go? I love this old place. Don't never think I can be happy no place else."

"But sooner or later someone will show up to claim ownership of this property. How do you know they'll let you stay here? Doesn't that bother you?"

"Reckon I don't never think about it a'fore. But I gotta stay here, you see. I gotta be close to my daddy and see after his grave. I's happy here, sir. There's much to do. I can't never go hungry. I can grow food, catch fish, cut wood. I can chop cotton and make my own clothes, sew 'em when they need mendin'." She clutched the Bible with both hands, as if she would lose it if she let go. "God looks after me, He does. I ain't got nothin' to worry 'bout."

She had spoken in a resolute tone, only it didn't make sense to him. Was it possible the young black girl was mentally ill? She seemed content with her life here, but that was all, with no plans for the future. He shut his eyes to relax, but reopened them when her next question startled him.

"Who's Alice?"

"Alice?"

"When you was sleepin', you was sayin' her name over 'n over."

"Are you sure?"

"Yes, sir."

He shook his head, saying, "I don't remember her."

"Maybe she's a girl you knowed at Vicksburg."

"I don't know that place," he said, though a voice inside him told him he did.

"You was sayin' Peter too, over 'n over." She paused for some reason, but then stepped away from the rocking chair and stood by the bed, peering down at him. "Was you speakin' 'bout Saint Peter, or is that your name? Is you called Peter, mista soldier?"

"To tell you the truth, I don't know *who* I am."

XI

"**H**ow long has you not knowed your name?"

"I'm not sure," Westmoreland answered her. "All I know is that when I woke up, I was lying next to a dead horse. There were five soldiers scattered around me. They were dead too. How I got there, I don't know." He shook his head. "I just don't remember."

"I heared you say Alice many times when you was sleepin'."

"Yes, you told me that before."

"I reckoned she was…" She hesitated.

"Yes?" he urged.

"Why, I…reckoned she was your wife. Is Alice your wife, mista soldier?"

"Don't know, Elsie, I can't remember."

"Reckoned she was your wife 'cause of that ring you been wearin'." She indicated the wedding band on his ring finger. "See."

He stared at the ring curiously, wondering how he hadn't noticed it before.

"Yes, I must be married," he said. Then he corrected himself. "No, I *am* married."

She was delighted and proved it with a gleaming white smile.

"Tell me more," she said. "You 'member what she looks like?"

"She's younger than I. She has long brown hair…and blue eyes. How I know that, I don't remember. But I do know it."

"Masta Jim had blue eyes, like his wife, Missy. My goodness, she had pretty eyes…and long hair. T'was long yellow hair. Missy was such a pretty picture in summertime. I 'member her wearin' them pretty party dresses and pink ribbons in her hair. My goodness, she loved pink ribbons, blue and white ones too."

"Tell me more about Colonel Madden," he said. "How long did he own this farm?"

"As long as I been here," was her answer. "T'was never round much the last few years. He was always ridin' to Richmond city and back. My daddy said he writ laws 'cause he's a smart man. A lawyer, he was."

"What was he like? How did he treat the coloreds?"

"T'was always good to me…and so was Missy," she said. "But Masta Jim could be a hard man when he had a mind to. I 'member the time old Rufus Cane run off with Missy's colt, Whisper. My daddy and the corn'l chased after him at the gallop. Rufus got three miles away a'fore they find him. My daddy had to punish Rufus for what he done."

"Oh, how?"

"He beat Rufus with a horse whip. Twenty times, I reckon it was. Masta Jim made us watch as my daddy took the whip to old Rufus. T'was an awful thing to see. Thought Rufus was gonna die. I didn't watch long, almost throwed up my supper. But my daddy said Masta Jim done the right thing. Learned Rufus a lesson, it did. And nobody never stole a horse from Masta Jim again."

"You seem to have much respect for Madden despite what you and the other coloreds were forced to do here."

"Reckon we just took things the way they was. Never knowed no other way to live. My granddaddy and his a'fore him was slaves. They's buried out yonder."

"Have you seen many soldiers?" was his next question.

"Some passed through when Masta Jim was here. But not too many come after that. Just a'fore the rest of the black peoples left, we was told the Yankee soldiers was comin'. You is the first one I seen, sir. If you stay here, I reckon the rest be comin' soon."

"No, I can't stay here," he told her. "I…have something important to do." He shook his head with emphasis. "Only I don't know what it is," he added glumly.

"Must be awful not knowin' what you is. How can you be sure 'bout anything?"

"My uniform proves who I am," answered the cavalryman. "Sooner or later I'll remember the rest."

She didn't say another word and left the shanty. He waited a few minutes, thinking she would be back. When she didn't, he climbed out of the bed, tried to stand, but quickly ended up on the floor.

When she returned later, she fed him warm soup she had made out of cornmeal, water and cereal grass, which he enjoyed and told her so. Afterwards he slept. It was another fitful sleep, during which his mind was bombarded with a variety of images: images of faces and events from his past.

He saw two boys. One, whose name was Peter, sported sun-bright yellow hair and a wide grin that seemed permanently glued to his face. The other was Peter's brother, whom Peter called Jon. Jon was thin-faced and fair of skin, was not as tall as his elder sibling. The two youngsters were sitting beneath a bright crescent moon and the sturdy limbs of a plump apple tree, laughing and singing together. Then, suddenly, they were running away from the orchard in fear of the bearded man with the funny black hat and pitch fork...

Another of the images in his dream was that of Jon and a young lady he called Alice. Alice was a pretty, slender woman who had big blue eyes and flowing dark hair the length of a sigh. They were standing together on a railway platform, watching as the steam locomotive braked into the station. Jonathan—that's what she called him—embraced her in a bear hug, as if never wanting to let go. But he did, leaving her behind sobbing as he climbed aboard the train…

The final image included Jon and two other soldiers dressed in blue uniforms. One was called Josh, the other Grant. Josh was Jon's friend and much younger than the bearded, plain-faced Grant. Words were bandied between them before Jon felt the strength of Mr. Grant's handshake and left the railroad car with orders to succeed in doing what needed to be done…

But what was it? What was Jon's duty?

Westmoreland awoke in a heavy sweat, the dream still loitering in his mind. He sat up in the bed feeling light-headed, but then fell back down, his eyes closing on impact. When he reopened them, Elsie was standing there.

Robert E. Lee had arrived in Hunter's Mill Tavern the day before with severe stomach cramps. The pain reminded him of his daily battle with diarrhea during the Gettysburg campaign. Colonel Walter Taylor, his aide-de-camp, suggested that he relax before supper, and Lee reluctantly agreed. The commander-in-chief donned his spectacles, opened his Bible and read the last two chapters of the Book of Revelation.

Later that evening, after dining with junior officers of a veteran Alabama infantry brigade, Lee met with Taylor and General James Longstreet in his quarters. Longstreet, a stout, unattractive man with a long nose and too much beard, commanded the celebrated First Corps of the Army of Northern Virginia. "Pete" Longstreet's Virginians had gained notoriety at the Second Battle of Bull Run in August '62, one of the South's greatest triumphs of the war. Yet history would remember Lee's "Old Warhorse" as the one who had ordered General George Pickett's infantry division to storm the impregnable Union center at Gettysburg, which ended in the loss of three-fourths of his command.

The meeting, however, was not about past glory or failures, but what to do about the army's future. Although Longstreet and Lee had great respect for each other, both had differing opinions at times on how best to conduct battle strategy and troop deployment. Both were proud, stubborn men, with Longstreet the more conservative of the pair. He was a procrastinator more times than he wasn't, unlike Lee who was confident in his ability to make decisions on the spot. Taylor, neutral in his role as Lee's adjutant, felt at times like a referee in a boxing match.

"I see no reason for you to go to Richmond," Longstreet told Lee tersely. The topic of discussion was the latter's scheduled meeting with Jefferson Davis in two days. "What purpose can it serve?"

"We need men, guns and more provisions I can count," was Lee's rejoinder. "I suspect the coming winter will not be a favorable one for the army. Meanwhile we must prepare for the spring. It is then when Grant will make his move against us."

"What makes you think he'll wait that long?"

"Because the rains have been particularly harsh this month," Lee reminded him. "Grant is not fully prepared to engage us at this time, especially in this godforsaken climate. Fortunately this respite has been a blessing for the army, allowing us to prepare for the attack which will come early next year. I just hope the president can afford me the extra troops and munitions."

"My men need food and better clothing to fight for you, General," countered Longstreet. "How long can we expect them to endure on the pitiful rations we give them? We have little meat, fresh fruit and vegetables. My troops wear rags for uniforms, and morale is low and getting worse each day."

Lee's eyes flared.

"I see no evidence of poor morale in the ranks!" he fired back. "The men know their duty. They've performed well in the past and will continue to do so in the months ahead. If we lose the war, it will be God's will, and not because the men did not do their best."

"Doing their best is not enough, General, and you know it. Grant has twice the number of troops and many more times that in munitions and food stores. You *must* face facts!"

"The men have endured these privations before, sir." Lee stared at an empty corner. "They will do their duty."

Longstreet shook his head, looking humbled, defeated. Taylor, who was standing next to him, decided it was a good time to intervene and voice his opinion.

"General Lee, with your permission?"

"Yes, Colonel Taylor?"

"Sir, perhaps General Longstreet has a solution to our problems, particularly with regard to our defenses at Richmond. Should we not at least hear him out?"

"Of course, Colonel." Lee turned. "General?"

"General Lee, you're well aware of my stand regarding our defenses at Richmond," said Longstreet. "This has not changed."

"You're still of the opinion that we should remove the army from the city and redeploy near Petersburg?"

"Yes, sir, I am."

Lee pursed his lips and thought about it, but not for long.

"No, sir," he said. "Although I respect your opinion, General, I will not abandon Richmond to those people. The city is in no imminent danger."

"But, General Lee, it is the opinion of my staff that Richmond is untenable against another attack, and that we must look to the threat to our supply lines. It's quite possible that Sherman will pull his army out of Georgia and march against our rear. He could force the issue even before Grant makes any kind of aggressive move. Petersburg is where we need to concentrate our forces."

"I beg to differ with you, General," said Taylor, butting in. "Reports from General Beauregard indicate that Sherman has only one corps ready to deploy and none in reserve. He said they've neither the stomach nor ambition to engage us at this time. We can hold Petersburg with what we have."

An awkward silence followed before Lee reclaimed the floor. He confronted Longstreet and dropped a comforting hand on his shoulder, surprising him. When he spoke, it was as if he were reciting sacred script from the Bible.

"General Longstreet, please be assured that I respect your opinion more than any other soldier in the army. I know you want only the best solution to the present crisis. However, please respect my opinion as well, for I, too, want only the best for our troops. We will speak more of this tomorrow."

He nodded. "Please feel free to retire."

Longstreet was at a loss for words, had nothing worthwhile to contribute. Reluctantly he donned his hat and gauntlets, clicked his heels together and raised his right hand to his hat. Lee returned the salute and watched as he left the building with his chin buried in his throat.

Later that night as he sat by the fireplace, Lee thought about his forthcoming meeting with Jefferson Davis. Would it be a profitable one? Would he get the troops and supplies he so desperately needed? Or would it be a waste of time as Longstreet had prophesized? Whatever the outcome, it didn't matter. His duty to Virginia was clear. He would never abandon her.

He opened the Bible and forced himself to read.

XII

To say that Claude-Henry Tombs grew up amid much privation and abuse would be a gross understatement. Born in a back street bordello in Baton Rouge, Louisiana, on the final hour of the last day of 1836, Hank Tombs had endured one hardship after another in what would be an abbreviated, troubled life.

He outlived his mother, an inexpensive whore of French ancestry who died after delivering her newborn into the arms of the child's aunt, her sister, who was also a member of the oldest profession. His father, a second-rate blacksmith by trade and skilled drunk by habit, convinced Hank at an early age that disobedience to his elder would not be tolerated. The old man made his point with his foul mouth and fists on more occasions than were necessary.

Not surprisingly, Hank ran away from home at the age of twelve, leaving his penniless father behind to wither away in loneliness and shame. To make it on his own, Hank became a street vagabond, panhandling for everything he needed to survive. It was inevitable that he would turn to a life of sin, for it was less than five months after he had left his father when he was arrested by a conscientious beat cop. His crime was larceny, the article in question a worthless stick pin owned by an elderly Spanish woman who died of a heart seizure while trying to keep it from him.

But he was "too young for jail," the judge pronounced at the hearing, and Hank was sentenced to do penance in a juvenile detention home run by a determined Roman Catholic priest and his complement of equally determined nuns. This lasted exactly two days before Hank got rabbit in his blood. For the next six years he went from more trouble to less sympathetic judges to harsher boarding schools before the parish authorities decided enough was enough. The boat which ferried eighteen-year-old Claude-Henry Tombs to the Louisiana state prison arrived at the dock on the afternoon of 22 September 1855.

By prison standards it was an unusual place. There was no stockade to stop the prisoners from running away, and only a dozen armed guards to keep it from happening. Escape seemed ridiculously too easy until Hank learned that the prison was situated on a former sugar cane plantation on an island in the middle of the bayou. The place was surrounded by an endless moat of disease-ridden swamp and guarded day and night by an undefeated army of alligators and poisonous water snakes.

Undeterred and willing to do anything to escape, many of the prisoners tried their luck but without success. Some vanished into the bowels of the swamp, never to be heard from again. The others, those lucky enough to be found and brought back to the prison alive, returned with permanent scars to remind them of their folly: insect bites; massive water boils; and missing body parts from hungry reptiles. Thus, with nowhere to go for the next six years, Hank Tombs had no choice but to modify his lifestyle.

But it was difficult. The mosquitoes were as large as sparrows, and the steady diet of rice and fish made mealtime just another routine chore. The veteran prisoners, the majority uneducated, hardened criminals, were in charge of the place. As a newcomer you either listened or were abused. For Tombs, it was like living with his father again, only a hundred times worse. Outnumbered and wanting to see the outside world again, Hank learned to swallow his pride and take orders from men who had been classified by society as the lowest form of humanity.

In March '61, Hank was released from prison. He was given new clothes and five dollars by the state, of which the latter he used to buy a ride on a riverboat to Memphis. There, Hank wandered around for a while before finding employment as a bellhop in a luxury hotel. Carrying bags and fetching things for the wealthy was menial, degrading work befitting of an ex-convict, but it was a job that kept him financially solvent and out of mischief.

On the seventh day of May of the same year, the great state of Tennessee entered into a military league with the Confederacy. This was followed a month later by a popular vote of two to one in favor of secession. Tennessee was officially at war with the United States of America. Like many others who saw the war as a once-in-a-lifetime opportunity, Claude-Henry Tombs abandoned the only steady job he had ever held and joined the newly hatched Confederate Army of Tennessee.

Incredibly enough, Hank found it easy adapting to army life. The food was better than anything he had tasted in prison, and the constant interaction of close comradeship was something he quickly learned to appreciate. Most amazingly was his tolerance for taking orders: a result of his "training" in the bayou. His adoption by the military went so well, he was promoted to corporal after only eight months of service, three weeks before he felt the first sting of battle. That happened at the infamous peach orchard in a place the Yankees called Pittsburg Landing. Their enemy called it Shiloh.

The constant flow of blood and the pervading stench from bloated, inert bodies was something he had never expected, nor would ever forget. The shelling from the massive Federal guns was almost more than a human being could take. During the battle Hank lost five buddies, of whom one had died in his own arms from the shrapnel of double canister the "blue bellies" were using. Mostly, he remembered not being able to hold anything in his stomach for several days after the engagement.

Following the Vicksburg debacle, Hank convinced himself that the war was a lost cause. High-ranking commanders were branded as scatterbrains, the same who had been touted earlier in the war as military geniuses. Desertions in the ranks swelled to epidemic proportions after word of Lee's defeat at Gettysburg was confirmed by the Yankee newspapers. The great cause of Southern independence had become a hopeless crusade. Sergeant Claude-Henry Tombs, a veteran of three major battles and countless insignificant skirmishes, knew he had to make a decision to save himself before it was too late.

He made up his mind for good just seven days before the bloodbath at Chickamauga commenced. For a man of limited intelligence, it was a well thought-out plan. Tombs, along with four others, volunteered for picket duty on the night of 31 August, bolted when the opportunity presented itself, and never returned for morning reveille. After a search party produced nothing later that day, the five were given up for good by the officer in charge, who listed them in the duty roster as "absent without official leave."

The deserters crossed into no man's land on 2 September. Without maps to guide them, Hank and his gang found themselves lost within a week. Worse, they had exhausted their rations and were desperately in need of rest and nourishment. Two of the men had contracted malaria and were left behind to fend for themselves. Finally, on the afternoon of the twenty-fifth, the renegade trio stumbled upon a wandering troupe of Negroes encamped near the Tennessee River, just within hollering distance of Knoxville.

The Mississippi blacks, who proudly called themselves free men, had escaped their cotton master in Jackson and were heading north for the better life promised to them by "Mista Linkum".

The opportunity was too obvious to ignore. The ex-Confederate soldiers robbed the former slaves of three horses and enough rations to sustain them for a fortnight's travel. From Knoxville the renegades crossed the Virginia border, looting whenever it suited them. Claude-Henry Tombs, who many times during his stay in prison had sworn to his Maker that he would never steal again, had returned to the ways of his adolescence.

By the spring of '64, their ranks had swollen to a baker's dozen. Most were army deserters, the rest mere cowards who had sidestepped military service. Ironically, one was a Yankee deserter from Maine who had been running and hiding ever since wandering away from the Antietam bloodbath in September '62. Self-appointed leader of the outlaws, Tombs spit out orders like a drill officer in charge of a rifle company. Whatever he said was law, no ifs, ands, or buts about it.

They even labeled themselves the Black Legion, though they were little more than petty thieves plundering the Virginia countryside and its unsuspecting citizens. Since Confederate money was all but worthless, they usually helped themselves to expensive personal possessions, in particular items of gold and silver. However, their good fortune came to an abrupt end on the day Hank Tombs made the worst decision of his life.

Confronted by a Confederate officer of distinction who

had been invalided out of the war due to an inoperable right arm and peg leg, Tombs shot the man at point-blank range for a silver pocket watch the ex-soldier had stubbornly refused to relinquish. Witnesses of the gruesome scene informed the authorities in charge of law and order, who in turn alerted the local militia. News of the cold-blooded murder made it all the way to the headquarters of General James Longstreet, whose aide-de-camp issued a directive that a substantial reward would be tendered to any man or group of men who captured or destroyed the Black Legion. The chase was on.

The renegades barely avoided capture near Spotsylvania courthouse by a wandering night patrol. They tried to seek sanctuary on the other side of the picket line, but their reputation had preceded them and they were chased away by a vociferous battery of Rhode Island sharpshooters. Four members of the Legion were cut down in the crossfire, with two others wounded beyond repair.

Their ranks having shrunk to seven, the outlaws split up in an effort to confuse the unrelenting hound. One group, four in all, headed back west for the Tennessee border, while the others, with Tombs in command, took the opposite route. For the latter part of the summer, Hank and his cronies were able to dodge and confound their enemy, but just barely. News of the others being apprehended, tried and hung reached Tombs while he and his gang were holed up in an abandoned lean-to in the war-weary town of Hopewell Station, Virginia. It was late in the evening of 30 October.

"Says in this here newspaper they was caught near

Petersburg," said Chud Culpepper. Culpepper was the youngest of the trio who, like Tombs, was an original member of the Black Legion. He stroked the length of his black beard. "Luke and the boys never had a chance," he added dolefully.

"Let me see that!" Tombs reached over and snatched the newspaper from him.

"But, Hank, you know you can't read."

"I ain't tryin' to. I just wanna see the pitcher."

Tombs frowned at the photograph of his former mates hanging lifeless from the gallows. Like slabs of beef in a slaughterhouse. He felt his stomach move.

"Ain't a pretty sight," he said unnecessarily.

"What are we gonna do now?" asked Fred Darling.

Tombs faced him. The deserter from Maine, Darling was standing in the opposite corner with his horse, feeding the animal something he was holding in his right hand. Darling was an immature twenty-two-year-old, a stick of a man who had a dirty habit of picking his nose whenever he was distraught or nervous. At that moment he was doing just that with the thumb and forefinger of his left hand.

"Don't know," Tombs answered him. "Reckon I just gotta think about it." He reached for the flask of whiskey beside him and yanked out the cork.

Culpepper said, "If I was you, I wouldn't take my time about it."

"Hush your mouth, Chud!"

"Maybe it's time we split up," suggested Darling, his words directed at Tombs.

"Now that's the dumbest thing I ever heared come out of

your mouth, boy, seein's what happened to Luke and the others. You wanna end up dead, like them?"

"But what are we gonna do?" Darling's face was a portrait of confusion. "We gotta have a plan."

"We keep moving," Tombs told him. "We'll hide the loot and head south, then do something they ain't never gonna think. We'll join the army."

Culpepper glared at Tombs as if he were deranged.

"Hank, did you say what I think you said?"

"You heared me right."

"You crazy or something?" The words were Darling's.

"Listen, boy, the best way to stop the army from lookin' fer you is to hide where they don't reckon you to be. We'll join the army at Petersburg. We'll turn ourselves in and tell 'em we escaped from Yankee prison."

"But what if someone spots us?"

"Who in hell's fire gonna do that?" said Tombs. "Anyhow, you got a better idea?"

"I say we keep moving," said Culpepper. "I don't fancy going back to the army. They might send us up to the front lines."

Tombs laughed at him.

"Would you rather die like Luke and the boys?" He raised the newspaper and showed the grisly photograph. Culpepper swallowed the stone in his throat.

"Reckon you're right," he said. "A bullet *would* be a might quicker."

Tombs swung his attention to Darling and found the Yankee coward sitting on his knees, holding a split hoof in his hands. It was the mare's left hind one.

"You hear me, boy?"

"Yeah, I heared ya." Darling stared at the hoof, shaking his head. "My horse is lame, Hank. She's got a broke foot."

"You and Chud will ride double till we find you another."

Culpepper said, "When we leavin', Hank?"

"Soon as we get some rest," was Tombs' reply. To Darling he said, "Any objections, boy, or do you wanna go back to your army instead?"

"No, Hank, no objections."

"Good, that's the way I like you, boy—scared to death. Trust me, you'll live longer if you stay that way." Tombs drank from the flask, laughed again, then lay down and closed his eyes. "Chud, take the first watch."

XIII

President Jefferson Davis and Robert E. Lee met in Richmond as scheduled on the morning of 31 October.

As it turned out, the meeting was a huge disappointment. Lee was told by the leader of the Confederacy that extra food supplies and munitions were "out of the question." In addition, most able-bodied men, both young and old, had already been conscripted into military service. To make matters worse, Federal naval blockades of southern ports continued to deny the South of vital war matériel from foreign powers sympathetic to the rebels' cause. However, the worst news of all had come from Georgia, where General William Tecumseh Sherman's army was still running amok, plundering and laying waste to the great state. "You must make do with what you have, General."

Following the meeting, Lee visited his home and spent the remainder of the day with his wife and family. Early the next morning he and his entourage left the capital to start the long journey back to Hunter's Mill Tavern. Upon their arrival in the town later that afternoon, Lee sent a runner to fetch General James Longstreet, who appeared in Lee's quarters just after dusk. Colonel Taylor was also in attendance.

"So there it is," Lee told them. "To say the least, the president painted a grim picture." He sighed. "May God help us."

Longstreet said, "Begging your pardon, sir, but we must take action and end the war. We can't rely on the men to make more sacrifices for a lost cause. It's insane!"

"It's not our decision," rebutted Lee. "As soldiers we must do our duty. And our duty is to Virginia and the president."

"Our duty, with all due respect, General, is to look after the welfare of our troops. We can't expect them to fight under these conditions forever. Winter is fast approaching. As you once said, it will no doubt be a bad one, perhaps worse than last year."

Ignoring him, Lee said to Taylor, "Colonel, I want to leave Hunter's Mill first thing in the morning. Please have Traveller saddled and ready by daybreak. We'll need to be in Willistown by nightfall. We'll spend two days there before returning to headquarters."

"Yes, sir."

Lee said to Longstreet, "And you, sir, must look to your corps. I've no doubt you will do your duty."

"General, in the name of God and all that is decent, please hear me out. You must finish this war now. You, and only you, have the power to end the senseless slaughter."

"No, I will not disobey a direct order from the president!" roared Lee. "We owe it to those who have given their lives to keep fighting. Since last spring, Grant has fought us many times and we've foiled him at every turn. His army has taken heavy losses, more than twice our numbers. It is the president's opinion that if we continue to thwart the enemy, those people will give up and seek a negotiated peace."

"But, General Lee, Grant can afford the casualties, we can't. Sir, I ask you one more time, I implore you—"

"Enough of this!" said Lee, cutting him off. "Rest assured that I respect your opinion, General, but the matter is out of my hands. Please leave now and return to your corps. It is there where you are needed, sir."

Silence.

Longstreet seemed ready to continue the debate, and for a brief moment Lee thought he would. Reluctantly the former chose not to, saluted and headed for the exit. When he was gone, Lee confronted Taylor, who thought his commanding officer looked tired, drained from the ordeal.

"Sir, are you all right?"

"I feel older, Colonel, much older."

"Perhaps you just need more rest."

Lee nodded feebly, then asked, "Colonel, what are your thoughts? Do you believe General Longstreet is right? Should we end the war now?"

"Sir, I respectfully decline to answer."

"Please, Colonel, I'd like to know your opinion."

"General Lee, my duty is to serve the army. I will do so until you decide otherwise. However…"

"Go on."

"Well, sir, I agree with General Longstreet. I believe we must end the war for the sake of our country and the people who have suffered on her behalf. It would be the honorable thing to do."

"Thank you for your honesty, Colonel." Lee flashed a smile. "Now then, is there anything else I need to do before I retire this evening?"

"Yes, General, there is." Taylor produced a pocket watch from his tunic, opened it and noted the time. "You have a meeting with Captain Anderson at nine o'clock, sir. That's five minutes from now."

"Yes, of course. Is the captain waiting outside?"

"Yes, sir."

"Very well. Tell him I'll receive him directly."

Taylor saluted and left the room. Not long thereafter Captain William Anderson appeared at the door. He marched into the room as if behind schedule, and Lee met him halfway. Anderson put his feet together with a thud and raised his right hand in salute. It was a brave, three-fingered salute, for he had lost his thumb and forefinger at the Second Battle of Bull Run in August '62. Lee returned the salute.

"Very good of you to come, Captain." He inadvertently glanced at Anderson's left sleeve, the one which was empty from the elbow down. That had happened at Bull Run as well: the result of a glancing blow from a Union cavalryman's saber. "I trust you are well, sir?"

"I am very well, thank you, General. Ready to serve."

"Please join me at the map table."

"A privilege, sir."

Lee offered Anderson the chair next to his. Smiling, Anderson sat down and waited for Lee to begin.

"It is so gratifying to see one of my most loyal intelligence officers again," Lee told him. "Colonel Taylor tells me you've been very busy."

"Quite true, sir."

"Very well, Captain, what new information do you have for me?"

"Tell me more about Colonel Madden and his family," Westmoreland asked Elsie after she had returned to the shanty on the evening of the thirty-first following a long day's worth of chores.

"Well, like I said a'fore, Masta Jim went away with the army and never come back."

"And you said he was killed near Richmond?"

"Yes, sir, in a great battle, we was told. When Missy heared about it, she lost her head. Tried to hang 'erself, she did. After that, she never been the same."

"What happened?"

"My daddy fetched the doctor and the doctor sent her away."

"Where?" he urged.

"The mountains, I reckon, with the rest of her family."

"And that's when the other coloreds decided to leave?"

"Yes, sir, all but me and my daddy…and some of the rest. But they went away too."

"I still can't believe no one has come here to claim ownership of this property," he said, shaking his head. "Is it because the land is no good?"

"No, sir, the land is very good. I grow things all the time. Like I said a'fore, we got visitors."

"Yes, you mentioned that gray soldiers had come to the plantation on several occasions. Tell me, what happened while they were here?"

"Not much," was her answer. "They was just here a day or two. They stayed in the big house, and I made them meals to eat. They was very polite to us. They took most of the grain and tobacco a'fore they went away. Two boys, Buster and Charlie, went away with 'em. They was going to fight in the army too."

"Two black men serving in the rebel army?" He grunted. "That's hard to believe."

"No, it's true, Jon."

It was the first time she called him by his Christian name ever since he had regained memory of it. That happened earlier in the day.

"Thank you for using my name, Elsie."

"Reckon you was able to 'member more? Sure would like to know more 'bout you, Cap'n Jon."

"'Fraid I don't have anything else to tell you. All I know so far is that I'm an officer in the Union army. But what I'm doing here is still a mystery to me. But I do know that I've something important to do, only I don't know what it is." A tired sigh before he added, "Guess it'll come back to me, like my name did."

"Sure hope so." She grabbed the tea kettle from the cooking stove, using an old rag as a pot holder. "Do you want some tea...or more rabbit meat?"

"No, thank you. But the meat was delicious." He lay down on the bed and smiled at the ceiling. "Tell me, Elsie, how did you learn to trap rabbits?"

"My daddy learned me."

"He must have been quite a man."

"My daddy was everything to me. He was..." She stopped herself for some reason, and he saw her eyes glistening in the firelight. Two bright stars in the night sky. "Please try to rest, Jon."

"You're right. Maybe it'll help my memory."

She watched him, waiting until his eyes were shut, and then left the shanty. Westmoreland heard the door close and reopened his eyes. He stared at the crack in the ceiling, wondering how much longer he could stay there. He was almost well enough to leave, only where would he go, back to the Union lines? No, he couldn't go back. He had something to do, something very important. But what was it?

Dear God, why can I not remember?

Hank Tombs, Chud Culpepper and Fred Darling left Hopewell Station the same morning Lee was in conference with Jefferson Davis. Their first priority was to find a replacement for Darling's horse, which they did just before noon. Darling's new mount, formerly owned by the daughter of an elderly Baptist minister in a small town they had never heard of, was a brown and white colt with plenty of spirit.

They rode at a steady pace for twelve hours, taking the long way around Richmond and barely avoiding contact with a rebel patrol. Then they headed east. Several miles later they found the road blocked by a munitions train, forcing them to take a more arduous rural route. As dusk approached, the scent of rain was heavy in the air. It began to drizzle when they saw the white mansion approaching in the distance. There were no lights in the windows.

"Looks empty," said Culpepper. He spit out used chewing tobacco and wiped his mouth with his sleeve. "What do you make of it, Hank?"

"It's dark everywhere," was Tombs' response.

"Looks like a good place we can rest a spell. Reckon there's food in the house?"

Before Tombs could answer him, Darling said, "I see smoke!" He indicated smoke of the gray variety climbing from the chimney of the first in a row of small hovels across the way. "Somebody's cooking, you smell it?"

"Yeah, I smell it," nodded Tombs.

It started to rain harder.

"Let's get out the rain!" howled an impatient Darling.

"Not so fast!" Tombs told him. "First we gotta have a plan."

"Come on, Hank, I'm gettin' soaked!"

"Easy, boy!" Tombs reached out and seized Darling's

reins. "Didn't you learn nothin' while you was in the army? It could be a trap. We'll scout the place a'fore we move in. Chud and me will go round back. You go round the front. And don't make no damn noise!" He pointed to an area across the field. "We'll meet over yonder, near that old shed behind the boneyard."

Culpepper said, "What if it *is* a trap?"

"Then we turn tail and ride like the wind." Tombs tapped his heels into the horse's flanks. "Let's go!"

XIV

Elsie was filling her teacup at the hearth, her back to a slumbering Westmoreland, when the door opened and the renegades burst into the shanty, pistols at the ready position. Startled, she spun around to see what the commotion was about and gasped at the sight of the two strangers, at the same instant losing her grip on the tea kettle. The sound of the kettle hitting the floor roused Westmoreland from his nap.

His head jumped off the pillow as if shot from a cannon, prompting the rest of him to follow. He scrubbed the sleep from his eyes, conscious of the new presence in the room, his sprinting heartbeat, and watched as the uninvited guests with the rain-soaked hats and gray coats came into focus. Both men, their unkempt faces showing much evidence of a long day in the saddle, reeked with the stench of tired horse.

"What is this?" he shouted at them. "Who are you?"

"Shut your mouth, soldier boy!" commanded Tombs.

Westmoreland was not listening. He hurled the blankets aside, swung his feet out of the bed and tried to stand, only Culpepper was too quick. The ex-soldier rushed in and showed Westmoreland his loaded horse pistol, forcing him to acquiesce.

"Easy, Colonel," he warned. "Take it easy and nobody gets hurt."

"That's right," added Tombs. "We ain't lookin' fer no trouble."

There was a victory smirk plastered to his lips as he turned and confronted Elsie. He looked her over, enjoying the terrified look on her face, then surprised her when he reached closer and grabbed her wrist with his free hand. He squeezed when she tried to break free, and she winced as a result; but she didn't cry out.

"Who lives here, girl?"

No answer.

Tombs squeezed.

"Well?" he demanded.

Again no answer. She just stood there trembling like a frightened squirrel, her wide, dark eyes a display of fear and contempt for him. To Westmoreland, she seemed on the verge of fainting, as if she already knew that what was about to happen to her would not be a pleasant thing. Annoyed by the silence, Tombs raised his pistol to her head and squeezed again, harder.

"Answer me, girl! Who lives here?"

"Nobody—just me."

"She's just a child, Hank," said Culpepper, lending his opinion.

Tombs released her with a shove and holstered the pistol. He gave himself a minute to survey the room, frowning at what he saw, then suddenly disappeared into the room next door. Upon his return, there was a satisfied grin showing through his wet beard.

"Four beds in there, but not much else," he told his partner. "Might be a good place to set and rest a spell."

"Sure could use it, Hank."

Tombs said to Westmoreland, "You got a name?"

There was no reply, and Tombs' scarred face turned blood red with anger.

"Tell me!" he shouted. "I ain't got all day!"

"My name is—"

"Madden!" said Elsie, cutting in. She stepped between them, facing the outlaw. "His name is Madden—James Madden to you, sir."

"I ain't talkin' to you!" Tombs pushed her aside as though she were made of feathers. "Was talkin' to you, soldier boy."

"Leave her alone!"

"Shut up!"

Ignoring him, Westmoreland made another bold attempt to stand, was almost there, but again it was Culpepper who persuaded him to the contrary.

"You don't listen so good, do you, Colonel?" He showed his pistol and smirked. "Reckon I won't be so polite next time."

Tombs said, "I'm still waiting fer an answer, soldier boy. You this Madden fellow she claims you is?"

Westmoreland answered with a nod.

"Well, Colonel, reckon I forgot my manners." Tombs embellished an insincere salute. "That better, *sir?*"

Just then the door opened, and Fred Darling stumbled into the shanty, chest heaving, as though he had been running for miles. His hat was soaked through to the scalp, and the gray poncho hanging from his shoulders streaked with beads of rain water.

"Run the horses in the barn like you told me," he said, addressing Tombs. He wrinkled his nose at the sight of Westmoreland, but then his mood changed when he saw Elsie huddled in the corner near the fireplace. "Well, well, look what we got here."

Tombs growled, "Thought I told you to keep an eye out, boy!"

"But, Hank, it's pouring outside. I'm tired of standing in the rain."

"Use your head fer once and find something to stand under. Chud will spell you in an hour."

Darling glared at his boss, thought about pursuing the debate, but knew from experience he'd never get his way. With reluctance he turned on his heels and left the hovel at the double quick, mumbling to himself along the way. Culpepper closed the door behind him.

"That kid been back-sassin' you all day, Hank. Maybe it's time we got shed of him."

"Let me worry 'bout him, Chud."

Tombs removed his coat, exposing his soiled gray uniform, and threw it on the table. There were three V-shaped stripes attached to each of his shirt sleeves, denoting his former rank. He stepped over to the cooking hearth and spread his hands over the fire, enjoying the pulsating heat.

"Who are you?" he heard Westmoreland say. "What are you men doing here?"

It was Culpepper who answered, "Let's get something straight, Colonel, *we* do all the talking."

"That's right, soldier boy." Tombs turned to Elsie. "Get some food on the table, girl, and let's be quick about it!"

She roasted a fat capon which was just enough to feed them, and they chased it with homemade apple cider, a recipe handed down to her by her late grandmother. Following dinner, Westmoreland was persuaded to give up the bed to Tombs. Darling, having been relieved of guard duty by Culpepper, was the last to satisfy his belly with meat and drink, though his mind was clearly on something else.

"You is a pretty one, girl." The lust in his voice was as obvious as the animal look in his eyes. "I want her, Hank."

"What you talkin' about, boy?"

"Ah, Hank, you know what I mean. I ain't had a woman for three months."

"Forget it, she's just a skinny kid. Won't be no pleasure in it."

"Ah, come on, Hank, after I'm done with her, you can have her for yourself."

"I ain't in the mood. Besides, she's a darkie. She ain't worth the trouble."

"But I ain't never had a black girl before. Might be fun."

A smirk wearing on his lips, Darling started toward Elsie with hands and mind ready for action, and Westmoreland had seen enough.

"Leave her alone!" he shouted after him.

Darling stopped his momentum and spun around, scowling at the cavalryman.

"You say something to me?"

"I said leave her alone!"

Tombs said, "You just don't get it, do you, Colonel? *I* give the orders round here."

"That's right," said Darling. "We do what we want, take anything we please. Ain't that right, Hank?"

Tombs ignored him; his eyes were focused on Westmoreland's.

"We know why we's here, Colonel, but let's talk about you fer a spell. Why you in this old shack livin' with this here darkie?"

It was Elsie who answered, "He was hurt in a great battle last summertime. Was sick too…lost his memory." It was as close to the truth as she dared, although Tombs appeared unconvinced.

"You don't look like you was wounded, Colonel. She tellin' a story?"

"No, it's true. I fell off my horse during a skirmish with a

Yankee patrol and landed on my head. I've just regained my memory."

"Glad to hear it," said Tombs with obvious insincerity. To Darling he said, "Fetch me some chewin' tobacco from my saddlebags."

"But, Hank, I—"

"Damn you, boy, I'm tired of you belly-achin' all the time! Now do what I say!"

Darling left the hovel in a huff and never heard Westmoreland say, "You don't seem to have much control over him, Sergeant. Tell me, how did you lose his respect?"

"He's a damn Yankee! He ain't got no respect fer nobody. That's why he run away from the army."

"And you and the other man deserted too?"

"Yeah, that's right. You see, before they drop me in the box, I'm gonna make a profit in this here world. I ain't aimin' to die fer a lost cause no more. I'll die fer *my* cause."

"They hang cowards like you and your friends."

"True, Colonel, but first they gotta catch us."

"Eventually they will. If not, the Yankees will."

"But they won't 'cause I got a plan."

Westmoreland waited, expecting Tombs to elaborate, but then the door opened and Darling reappeared. He gave Tombs the pouch of chewing tobacco, then showed him the blue uniform he had brought along with him.

"Look what I got, Hank."

Tombs squinted at Westmoreland's uniform.

"Where d'ya find that, boy?"

"Chud found it hanging in the horse barn. Said you should

know about it."

Tombs grabbed the uniform from him, noting the shoulder bars with interest.

"A captain's uniform," he said to no one in particular.

"Can't see how that got here, Hank. We gotta be twenty miles from the picket lines."

"Might'a been left behind by a raiding party, or maybe..." Tombs stopped his voice and turned, facing Elsie. "Where'd this come from?"

No answer.

"I asked you a question, girl!"

Again no response, and Tombs lost his patience. He jumped off the bed mumbling obscenities, started toward her, but stopped halfway when Darling assumed the initiative. He moved in fast, forcing her back against the wall, grabbed her shoulders and shook.

"Tell him, girl, who belongs to this uniform?"

"Leave her alone!" Westmoreland shouted at him.

"Shut up! I don't take no orders from you!"

"But she doesn't know a thing—I swear!"

"Then supposin' you tell us," said Tombs. "Where'd this here uniform come from?"

"I...took it off a dead Yankee at Gettysburg."

"What fer?"

"Wanted it as a souvenir. We'd just won a skirmish with the blue bellies, and I brought it home to show my wife."

"What wife you talkin' about?"

"Maybe the darkie's his wife," said Darling, chuckling.

"Hush your mouth!" Tombs told him. To Westmoreland

he said, "You never told me you got a wife. Where is this woman?"

"She died," said Elsie, grabbing the outlaw's attention. "Buried her myself."

Tombs seemed skeptical.

"She tellin' the truth, Colonel?"

"Yes, my wife died a month ago. She was sick with malaria."

Darling said, "Don't believe him, Hank."

"Shut up!" Tombs yelled back. To Westmoreland he said, "You say you was at Gettysburg?"

"That's right, served with Jeb Stuart's cavalry."

"Yeah, I heared of him. Wasn't he kilt?"

Westmoreland nodded, remembering he had read somewhere that Stuart had met his demise at the Battle of Yellow Tavern. How he knew that, though, was a mystery.

Tombs said, "I heared Gettysburg was the worst of 'em all. How many men did you lose there, Colonel?"

"'Bout half my regiment."

The moment he finished, Chud Culpepper appeared in the shanty carrying two long-necked bottles with him, one in each hand.

"Look what I found, Hank." He showed the bottle in his left hand, but lost it when Darling suddenly reached in and liberated it from him.

"Jesus, it's wine!"

Tombs appropriated the other bottle and proceeded to wipe away the dust hiding the label. He grinned.

"Where'd you find 'em, Chud?"

"Found 'em while I was rootin' around in this here shed behind the big house. They was hidin' under some old tools."

"Any others there?"

"Hell, yeah, must be eight or nine more." Culpepper reclaimed the bottle from him. "Your turn for guard, Hank, I need some rest."

Tombs reluctantly gave his consent with a nod, then looked at Darling to see what he was up to. The coward from Maine had already uncorked the bottle and was sampling his first mouthful. He coughed when the robust liquid reached his stomach.

"Mighty fine," he said. "Tastes like blueberries."

Tombs said to Culpepper, "Keep an eye on the boy." He pointed at Westmoreland. "And keep the other one on the colonel. I don't trust him."

"Sure nuff, Hank."

Grinning like a gator, Tombs turned and marched out the door.

XV

During his brief and turbulent tenure as an adult, Fred Darling had never experienced the taste of wine. As part of an outlaw gang constantly on the run, he had sampled various brands of beer and homemade spirits pilfered in transit, but never fine, southern-aged wine. At first the dark liquid was much to his liking. "Like sweet cider," he told Chud Culpepper. Later, when the alcohol grabbed hold of him, he became a different person. His body language was more animated, and the words that rushed out of his mouth made little or no sense. Culpepper thought his comedy act was harmless entertainment. To Westmoreland, he was a slow-burning fuse.

By then he had hoped the wine would have overwhelmed Darling and put him to sleep, and yet there was no sign to indicate that it would happen anytime soon. Worse, Darling had begun to show renewed interest in Elsie and much less in his bottle. He wore a hungry animal-like face, which meant he had but one thing on his mind. A distraction was in order.

"What part of Maine are you from, son?"

Darling's nostrils flared like an angry bull's as he turned his eyes of hate to Westmoreland.

"Who you callin' 'son'?"

"Was talking to you, Private." Westmoreland exaggerated a fake grin. "I'm curious to know where you lived before the war started."

"Don't waste your time with him, Colonel," cut in Culpepper. "He's so dumb, he don't remember."

"I ain't dumb!" Darling growled back. "I just ain't had no proper schoolin'."

"Why did you join the army?" was Westmoreland's next question.

"'Cause I had to. My big brothers joined up, and I had to live up to 'em. Didn't wanna be branded a coward."

"But you *are* a coward. You deserted the army and now you're a wanted outlaw. Tell me, why did you do it? Were you scared of dying?"

"I ain't scared of nothin'!" Darling lashed back. "I'm gonna be important sum day, you'll see. I'm gonna be rich, I'm gonna be famous, I'm gonna be—"

"Ah, hush your mouth!" barked Culpepper. "I'm tired of

hearin' you talk big. You ain't never gonna be nothin'."

"No, you is wrong, Chud. I'm gonna do it sum day, you'll see."

"Sure, kid."

Ignoring him, Darling lifted the wine bottle to his mouth and swigged. When he pulled the bottle away, wine dribbled from the corners of his mouth. He cleaned his face with the back of his hand, then turned and faced Elsie. She was exactly where he had last seen her, sitting alone in the corner opposite Madden, an arm's length from the fireplace.

He said, "You think I'll be important sum day, don't you, girl?"

Nothing came out of her mouth.

"Well, don't you?" he urged.

More silence.

When nothing continued to happen, Darling stood out of the chair too fast and staggered as he took a step in her direction. He waited until the floor stopped teetering before trying his next step. Watching him, fearing the worst was about to happen, Westmoreland made a quick decision.

"*I* think you can be important someday," he said, snatching the young renegade's attention. "You can be anything you want if you put your mind to it."

"You is absolutely right, Colonel. Supposin' I can be president sum day."

Grinning, Darling resumed what he had been doing, but didn't get very far when he lost his balance and toppled to the floor, ending up on his hands and knees. Culpepper laughed as he struggled to pick himself up.

"You dumb kid, how you gonna be president? You can't even walk straight."

"Don't laugh at me, Chud!"

"Shut up!"

"No, I mean it! If you don't leave me alone, I…I'll kill you!"

Culpepper threw back his head and laughed harder.

"That's funny, kid. You couldn't kill a butterfly if it landed on your nose." He grabbed his bottle and drank. "Yeah, you is just a scared coward."

"I'll tell Hank what you called me."

"So what? He ain't here."

"Hank cares about me." Darling made his way back to the chair and sat down, rubbing his throbbing forehead. "Yeah, Hank cares about me. He'll show you a thing or two."

"Got news fer you, kid. Hank Tombs don't care 'bout nobody but hisself. When you gonna learn that?"

"No, he cares about me, Chud. Just ask the Colonel, he'll tell you." He glanced at Westmoreland for effect. "Ain't that right, sir?"

There was no comment in return, just more of Culpepper's sarcastic laughter.

"Yeah, you is just dumb, kid," he said to his bottle.

"No, I'll show you, Chud. I'm gonna do anything I want. And nobody ain't never gonna stop me." Darling rose from his seat and headed toward Else again, this time with more speed in his step.

"Leave her be!" Culpepper shouted behind him.

"I don't take no orders from you!" Darling yelled back,

without turning around.

"I said, leave her be!" Culpepper jumped to his feet and started after him. He stopped when Darling spun around, showing his revolver.

"I told you, Chud, leave me alone or I'll kill you!"

"Look, kid, we don't need no trouble tonight. Leave her be, I say."

"So you want her for yourself, huh? Well, you can't have her—she's mine!" Darling squinted at Elsie, wearing that starving animal look again. "You can have her when I'm done with her."

"No, kid!"

Darling was not listening. He lunged at Elsie, she screamed, and Westmoreland did not hesitate.

He vaulted to his feet and charged Darling with hands extended, ready to destroy. He might have succeeded had it not been for Culpepper. The outlaw pistol-whipped him from behind, just above the neckline, and the Pennsylvanian crashed to the floor like a sack of flour, already unconscious, a thin line of blood trickling from his new wound.

Culpepper roared, "You dumb fool, look what you made me do!"

But Darling had not heard him, was too busy holstering his revolver. Finished, he went after Elsie and trapped her in the corner, grabbed her with both hands and shoved her into the room next door. Laughing, he stumbled in after her, and the door closed behind him.

Culpepper thought about going in after him, but decided instead it wasn't worth the effort. He grabbed his bottle from the table and finished what was in it. He waddled around the room for a while, not sure what to do, then flopped down on the chair Darling had vacated. He grabbed the other bottle, lifted it to his mouth, drank air, cursed, tossed the bottle into the fireplace, heard it shatter, and forced himself to ignore her screams.

Elsie fought Darling the best she could, only he was much too strong for her. As it turned out, the whole dastardly act lasted barely eight minutes.

From the very beginning Darling was clumsy, seemed to have no idea what he was trying to accomplish. Eventually he stripped her of her trousers, pinned her against the floor, and found what he wanted. Finished, he somehow managed to pick himself off the floor, struggled to button his trousers, fell, stood again, and lunged for the door handle before he fell again. After several attempts he opened the door and stumbled out of the room, leaving her behind sobbing on the floor.

Culpepper, still sitting at the table, involved in his own world of misery, did not utter a sound when Darling reappeared with a sleepy grin glued to his lips. He nearly tripped over the prostrate Westmoreland, somehow made his way to the bed, and collapsed head first on the mattress. He was asleep almost instantly.

Culpepper, not far from the edge of intoxication, watched Darling until he got tired of it. He glanced at Madden, wondering if he should try to help the man. Deciding at last he had neither the energy nor the medical know-how, he slumped over the table and closed his eyes.

It was a miracle Elsie had not been hurt during the sordid ordeal. "An act of God," she would tell herself later. She cleaned up afterwards the best she could and climbed into her trousers. When she exited the room, she was stunned at the picture she saw. She should have grabbed one of their guns and shot the renegades while they slept, but the thought never crossed her mind. In fact, her first reaction was instinctively maternal. After she had finished examining the wound, she rushed back to the other room, found a kerchief to use as a head bandage, and returned to Westmoreland's side.

As she started to dress the wound, Hank Tombs burst into the shanty like a gust of angry wind, startling her. He was panting wildly, the color on his face deathly pale as he studied the bizarre scene in front of him. The fit-to-be-tied mood in his eyes proved he was not happy about it.

"Jesus!" was the first word that spat out of his mouth.

He stepped up behind Culpepper and shook him, then again with more venom. Slowly, Culpepper raised his head and squinted at his blurry associate.

"Hank?"

"What happened here, Chud?"

"Ah, it was the kid, Hank. He went crazy wild. Took the girl in the back room and..." He sighed. "I told him not to do it, but he was drunk, wouldn't listen to me."

Tombs pointed at Westmoreland. "What about him?"

"The colonel tried to stop him, so I had to knock him down with my pistol. Reckon I hit him too hard."

"We gotta get out of here, Chud."

"What do you mean?"

"I heared horses down the road. Reckon they ain't no more than a mile away. I got the horses saddled. Let's go!"

"What about the kid, Hank? I say we leave him here to rot. He ain't nothin' but trouble no more."

"No, we can't. If they find him, he'll tell 'em our plan."

"Yeah, reckon you're right."

Tombs circled round the table and stood by the bed, glowering at the sorry portrait of Darling sprawled across it. He reached down and grabbed him by the nape of his collar.

"Wake up, boy!" Tombs rolled him over and slapped his face. "On your feet!"

Darling's eyes opened, he squinted, and Tombs came into focus.

"What is it? What's going on?"

"I said on your feet!" commanded Tombs with a voice angrier than the last one. "Horse soldiers is comin' this way fast. Now get up, we gotta leave!"

"I don't hear nothin'."

"Look, boy, I ain't got no time to jaw with you. If we don't leave now, they'll find us here. When that happens, they'll hang us fer sure." Tombs dragged him out of the bed. "Let's go!"

Culpepper said, "What about the colonel, Hank…and the girl?"

"We ain't got no time to worry about 'em. We gotta get out of here a'fore it's too late."

"I don't feel so good," mumbled Darling, clutching his

stomach. "Don't think I can make it."

Hank Tombs lost his temper then.

"Listen to me, boy, and listen good! If you stay here, they'll kill you fer sure. If you don't come along, I'll kill you myself! Got it?"

"Sure thing, Hank." Darling looked as terrified as his voice sounded. "I'll make it."

Culpepper led the way out, Tombs trailing behind him. Still woozy from the wine and his sexual feat, Darling started after them but tripped and fell, landing awkwardly on his side. Back on his feet, he steadied himself somehow and reached for the door handle, unaware that his left arm was broken in two places.

"Don't leave me, Hank!"

Outside, he heard the waning sounds of galloping horses. He stared in that direction, hoping to catch a glimpse of his partners, but they were not there, had vanished into the dusk.

"Hank!"

But there was no answer, couldn't be.

Darling searched for and found his colt tethered to a tree nearby, waiting for him. His head was a dervish of pain as he grabbed hold of the reins and stepped into the stirrup. He paused to throw up his wine and supper, mounted after several failed attempts, vomited again and punched his heels into the animal's sides.

XVI

It was a quarter hour after Tombs and his cohorts had left the plantation when Elsie heard the ominous noise of rifle fire in the distance. Ten minutes later the gun battle ended. The reign of terror known as the Black Legion was over.

Ironically, Fred Darling, the last to leave the farm, was the first one cut down by the horse soldiers' deadly crossfire. Hit thrice below the chest, he experienced a slow, agonizing death. Although his partners survived the initial onslaught, their fate was never in doubt. They were tracked down two miles west of the Madden property line and cut off from escape when they reached the riverbank.

Chud Culpepper died taking a shot in the head while trying to cross the river. Tombs, who had never learned to swim, had no choice but to shoot it out with his foe and was captured after his last round was spent. The following morning he was tried by an unforgiving military court, sentenced and hanged for his many crimes before eighty-five spectators, all of whom proudly wore Confederate battle gray. His last words in life, according to eyewitnesses, were dedicated to his mother whose French name he mispronounced.

Jon Westmoreland awoke on the morning Claude-Henry Tombs went to meet his Maker after spending a fitful night recovering from his head wound. Not surprisingly, he had a splitting headache. The first thing he saw when he opened his eyes was Elsie staring down at him, her wide eyes anxious, full of concern.

"You all right, Cap'n Jon?"

"Yes, I…think so." He flashed a courageous smile. "What about you? Are you all right?"

She nodded in answer, knowing he was referring to her ugly incident with Darling.

"I'm glad," he said.

She leaned closer and examined the head bandage, making sure it was doing its job.

"You need more rest," she told him.

She kept the fire going to keep him comfortable while he slept, but by late afternoon he was still asleep, and she began to worry that he might never recover. She prayed for him during the night, beseeching God to intervene on his behalf, and was oblivious of the fact she had not consumed a solitary morsel all day.

Westmoreland awoke just after dawn and found her asleep in the rocking chair, the Bible open across her lap. He sat up in the bed, both feet touching the floor, and tested the head wound. He felt pain when he applied pressure to the spot, but it was tolerable, nothing like the kind he had experienced the day previous. Slowly, he rose out of the bed, the floor teetered, and the inevitable followed. The noise he made hitting the floor brought her awake instantly.

"Jon!" She sprang from the rocker and helped him back into bed. "Stay here—please!"

"No, I've work to do, Elsie. I must leave."

"But you ain't done bein' sick. Anyhow, where was you aimin' to go?"

"Don't know, but I can't stay here."

"But they ain't round no more, you is safe here. They ain't never comin' back."

"How do you know that?"

"'Cause I heared shootin' last night," she answered. "I...think they was kilt."

"But that means there must be soldiers nearby." He pursed his lips in a show of defiance. "No, I can't stay here...and neither can you."

"But where do I go? I can't never leave here. This is my home, you see." She shook her head with emphasis, her version of defiance. "No, I can't never leave. I won't!"

"But what if they weren't killed? What if they come back? Look at the horrible things they did to you. Don't want that to happen again, do you?"

"But it won't, I tell you! Please believe me!"

He swung his eyes away from her, too tired to further the debate, and spotted his uniform sitting on one of the chairs at the table.

"I need my uniform back," he told her. "I can't wear Madden's anymore. I must leave this place."

"Why?"

"'Cause I've something important to do and it can't wait."

"But if you wear them clothes again, you'll be kilt when they find you. Wearing Masta Jim's clothes saved your life a'fore."

"I was lucky—and you know it." He sighed tiredly. "No, I must have my uniform back, I've a job to do."

"But I tell you, you ain't done bein' sick. You stay here so I can see after you." She turned to leave, but stopped when he grabbed her by the arm and pulled her back.

"Elsie, you must listen to me. I'm very grateful for your help. You saved my life twice. But I must leave this place, I've important work to do."

"How do you know that?"

"'Cause I remember everything now. I don't know how it happened or when, but I know who and what I am. I know why I was sent here."

"You sure?"

He took a slow, deep breath and said when he exhaled, "My full name is Jonathan Westmoreland. I'm a cavalry officer of the Thirteenth Pennsylvania Regiment. I was sent here on special orders by General Grant."

"Who…is Gen'l Grant?"

"He's the commanding general of the Union army. General Grant takes his orders directly from President Lincoln."

She squinted at him, obviously perplexed, so he told her the whole story of why he was there, including what had happened to him before she found him lying unconscious by the brook.

She said, "All the others was kilt?"

"Yes, I remember the incident now as if it were yesterday. I even remember the names of my men. Sean O'Grady. Billy Flanagan. Shorty Jones. Jake Carson. Zack Miller." He dropped his chin and added, "They were young men—all of them."

"Must'a been an awful thing to see."

"Yes, it was." He stared at her sad eyes. "So you see, Elsie, I must finish what I came here to do."

"But how you gonna do it? You can't stand up on your feet."

"I'll make it somehow, don't you worry."

"But I don't understand. Why is killin' Gen'l Lee so important?"

"Because Lee commands the Confederate army in Virginia. He makes all their battle decisions. Lee is the reason we've been unable to whip his army." She was still wearing the bewildered face, and he carried on, "Don't you see, Elsie? Too many men have died in this war. And many more will die if I don't do my duty. And my duty is to kill General Lee and end the war."

"I don't see how killin' one soldier can stop the war. How can you be sure?"

"Actually I'm not. We can only hope the enemy will give up when Lee is dead."

"But I can't believe you wanna kill him." She shook her head. "No, you just ain't the kind of man to do it."

"Tell you the truth, I don't like the idea of killing him either," he said to the floor. "I met General Lee once and have great respect for him. In fact, I'm not so sure I could pull the trigger if I got the opportunity to shoot him. I've asked myself that question a hundred times, but I still don't have an answer."

"So why do it?"

"Because it's my duty as a soldier."

She watched as he struggled to stand. He made it two steps before losing his balance. She helped him back to his feet.

"See what I mean?" She had spoken as if scolding a wayward child. "Please stay, Cap'n Jon."

He was too weary to continue the argument. Instead, he lay down on the bed and fell asleep. She waited, making sure, then collected his uniform and disappeared into the room next door, where she hid the clothes under the mattress of the bed furthest from the door. Later that morning when he woke up, she made a pot of tea and fried eggs for him, which he consumed with enthusiastic speed. An encouraging sign.

The new visitors arrived at the plantation as she was fixing him another cup of her dandelion tea. Like Tombs and his gang, the newcomers arrived by stealth, unannounced. They crowded into the shanty with pistols drawn and ready for action. And there was something very professional in the way they went about it.

There were four in all. Each soldier wore soiled battle gray and a tired face badly in need of a barber's razor. A fifth man, an officer with the rank of major, followed them into the shanty seconds later. He was the shortest of the intruders, no more than five-feet-five, Westmoreland estimated: a trim, fair-haired man whose chiseled facial features failed to disguise the dashing handsomeness of his youth. Unlike his colleagues, he wore a gray riding cap garnished with a fiery red feather, another symbol of his command authority. Along each side of his blue-gray trousers was a white stripe that started at the waist and stopped where the cotton fabric disappeared. More evidence that told Westmoreland he was a horse soldier, the pride and elite of the Confederate army.

The rebel officer scanned the room, his blue eyes missing nothing. His manner was that of a determined predator. But unlike his facial expression and rugged demeanor, his voice was calm and pleasant to the ear, like a pastor preaching Sunday sermon. His words were directed at Westmoreland.

"My apologies, Colonel." He looked the Pennsylvanian over, noting the head bandage with concern. "My name is Gibson—Major Matthew Gibson, of the First Virginia Cavalry." Smiling, he brought his boot heels together and saluted. "At your service, sir."

The history of Matthew Gibson was one that could have been conceived by a romantic novelist of the period. Gibson's great-grandfather was an English immigrant who had served in the ranks of George Washington's Continental army and died at Yorktown in what turned out to be the last great battle of the Revolution. The third of his four grandsons, Nathan Wayne, a lawyer by trade and member of the Virginia state legislature, had wanted his only son, Matthew Wayne, to follow in his path and devote his life to public service. As it turned out, his son obliged him, only not in the way the old man had hoped.

Wayne Gibson—he preferred not to be addressed by his Christian name—wanted to be a soldier. He loathed politics, partly because he had been exposed to it at an early age, but mostly because of the phony lifestyle associated with it. Work that included exhausting filibusters and formal affairs in high society wearing shirt collars that choked a man was not for him. A brilliant student who could have been a scholar and pursued almost any professional career, Gibson wanted his world to be filled with constant excitement and adventure. Contrary to his father's wish, which was a law degree from William and Mary College, Wayne opted instead for the United States Military Academy at West Point.

During his plebe year it became apparent that he would succeed in pursuit of his dream. He excelled in engineering, mathematics, literature, and most forms of athletic endeavor. By his third year he had earned the respect of his classmates and the majority of the army faculty who were astute enough to recognize his many talents. At his graduation in '59, Gibson was at the head of his class, a proven leader who would, in the words of one of his peers, "guide the army to victory in the next war for the glory and honor of the country." Lieutenant Wayne Gibson, an expert horseman at the age of twenty-one, decided he was best suited to serve in the cavalry corps. Two years later he was compelled to make a more difficult decision. The reason was a place called Fort Sumter, South Carolina.

On 17 April 1861, by a vote of 103 to 46 in the state legislature and later ratified by a four to one popular vote, the great Commonwealth of Virginia became the eighth state to secede from Abraham Lincoln's rapidly shrinking republic. At the time, Gibson was serving in Texas and did not receive word of his state's action until early May. After a difficult night's struggle with his conscience, he marched into the headquarters of his commanding officer, saluted as he always did, and with tears in his eyes and a trembling voice resigned his commission in the United States Army.

His rank and reputation preceding him home, Gibson accepted a new appointment with the rank of captain in Jeb Stuart's First Virginia Cavalry. During the next three years he survived one frying-pan battle after another. He served with distinction at the first Bull Run, where his daring cavalry charge routed a fixed enemy position. In December '62, he led a flanking attack against the Federal right at Fredericksburg which helped turn the tide and claim for the Confederacy its greatest victory of the war. Following the debacle at Gettysburg, where he had been wounded for the first time, Gibson rejoined his regiment after spending three difficult months in hospital.

By then, Ulysses S. Grant, now in supreme command of

the Union forces, assumed the initiative in what would become known in the history books as the Battle of the Wilderness. Restricted to defensive tactics, the First Virginia Cavalry contented themselves with hit-and-run raids to offset the enemy's superior numbers. Major Matthew Wayne Gibson, who had witnessed the bloodbaths at Spotsylvania and Cold Harbor, knew that the outcome of the war was but a foregone conclusion. Despite that, he stubbornly refused to abandon his duty, was still revered as a hero by those he led into battle…

Nearly a half minute had passed before an anxious Jon Westmoreland regained his poise and bravely returned the rebel major's salute. Still grinning, Gibson apologized again for the intrusion, barked out a command and exited the shanty in the same manner he had entered, his men following in his wake.

XVII

The picket soldiers were not at their best. One reason for it was the biting chill in the air which had settled over the area the night before, leaving a blanket of morning frost behind. Another was the outright complacency of the soldiers, a phenomenon in war caused by the lack of battlefield activity. Thus no one was prepared when the flag of truce appeared in the distance. The soldiers were more interested in their warm coffee cups.

It was nearly a minute later when young Albert Hayes, having laughed at something someone had said, spotted the white flag bobbing through the foliage. About fifty yards away, he estimated. At first he thought he was seeing things. When the flag suddenly disappeared from view, he was convinced that it had been a mirage and went back to his coffee. When he looked again, the white flag had magically reappeared, this time accompanied by two men dressed in gray uniforms. The one not hefting the flag was an officer, he was certain. He nudged the man crouched beside him at the campfire.

"Guess what, Sergeant, we got visitors."

Peter Wilson grunted, annoyed by the interruption. He placed the coffee pot on the makeshift rock stove while nervously stroking the end of his handlebar moustache with his free hand. When he looked up, the flag of truce had disappeared.

"I don't see nothin'."

"There, Sergeant." Hayes stood and indicated what he meant, and Wilson rushed to his feet.

"Well, what do you know, Hayes, you're right. Looks like we got us two more rabbits this morning." Wilson beckoned Hardy Jenkins, who was crouched beside him, poised to take a bite out of the warm biscuit in his hand. "Go see what those Johnny Rebs want, Corporal."

Reluctantly Jenkins did as he was told and moments later returned with the enemy soldiers. The one toting the flag was a young man, noted Wilson. The other man, an officer with the rank of lieutenant, carried a pair of tan saddlebags and seemed not much older than his compatriot. Wilson saluted.

"Good morning, Lieutenant," he said, trying to sound cheerful. "What can I do for you, sir?"

"My name is Crenshaw," said Crenshaw. He indicated the campfire with a nod. "Reckon you could spare some hot coffee, Sergeant? Smells awfully good from here."

"Sure thing, sir."

Wilson barked. Crenshaw took the cup from Hayes when it was offered to him and smiled gratefully in return.

"Much obliged, Private." He sipped, and his white smile broadened. "Reckon this'll take the chill out of the bone."

Wilson said, "So what brings you to my picket line, Lieutenant?"

Anthony Crenshaw, a native of the southeast Virginia seaport of Norfolk, enjoyed another swallow of coffee and told Wilson why he was there. When he was finished, Wilson caressed the other end of his moustache as he started a slow pacing routine, back and forth like an expectant father.

Jenkins said to Wilson, "What are you gonna do, Pete? That's one helluva cock 'n bull story."

Wilson stopped pacing and faced the rebel officer.

"You sure 'bout this, sir?"

"As God is my witness," Crenshaw told him. He finished the coffee and returned the cup to Hayes. "Thanks again, Private."

Jenkins said, "It must be true, Pete. Why else would they be here, except to surrender?"

"We're not here to surrender," Crenshaw corrected him. "My duty was to deliver the message, nothing more. Under a flag of truce, you're obliged to release us." To Wilson he said, "Do I have your word, Sergeant?"

"Yes, sir."

Crenshaw pointed to the saddlebags.

"Inside are the personal effects of the five men who were killed in the ambush." He flipped the saddlebags over, showing the initials *JW* branded in the leather. "We believe these saddlebags belonged to the officer in charge," he said. "Though his horse was shot out from under him, we never found his body."

Wilson opened the saddlebags and examined the contents. Among other things commonly associated with horse soldiers, there were three wrinkled maps neatly folded, a pair of field glasses, a handful of beef jerky wrapped in burlap, a compass, and a silver pocket watch. Wilson opened the cover and read the inscription on the reverse side. He looked at Crenshaw.

"Lieutenant, I'd be obliged if you'd stay a while longer. I want you to meet my commanding officer."

"Very well, Sergeant, but only on one condition."

"Sir?"

"Breakfast," said the rebel. "Private Joyce and I are famished. We've not had a hot meal since supper last night."

Wilson burst into laughter.

"Sure, why not?" he said. "We can offer you Johnny Rebs bacon and eggs, fresh biscuits with apple butter, and all the coffee you can swallow." He smiled proudly, adding, "Compliments of the Sixth New Hampshire Volunteers."

Colonel Thomas Pinckney studied the contents of the saddlebags for what seemed like an eternity. He glanced at Wilson who was staring back, then at Crenshaw who was doing the same. The rebel lieutenant was holding a tin cup of hot coffee, seemingly content in his new surroundings. Pinckney pointed to a spot on the map.

"You said the ambush took place *here*, Lieutenant?"

"That's right, Colonel. The officer in charge was a man named Marsh. According to his report, the ambush was well executed. He didn't lose a single man during the skirmish. I had the unpleasant task of being in charge of the burial detail."

"And you're absolutely certain there were no survivors?"

"Yes, sir."

Pinckney's aide, Bernard Woodside, who stood at the opposite side of the map table, said, "But, Lieutenant, you just told us the saddlebags belonged to an officer whose body was never recovered."

"That's right."

"Then it's possible he's still alive?"

"Yes, quite possible."

Pinckney said, "I want to thank you, Lieutenant, for coming here to tell me this information. Under the circumstances, it was the honorable thing to do."

"Your army would have done the same had the situation been reversed." Crenshaw pursed his lips. "A terrible thing this war, Colonel."

"Agreed." Pinckney turned around, facing Wilson. "Sergeant, have Lieutenant Crenshaw and the other man escorted back across the picket line."

"Yes, sir."

Crenshaw shook hands with Pinckney, thanked him again for his hospitality, saluted and marched out of the map room,

Wilson trailing at his heels. Pinckney's eyes met Woodside's.

"Well, Bernie, what do you think?"

"Not sure, Tom. I don't recall any patrols leaving here recently."

"No, you're wrong, there was one about a week ago. A six-man cavalry detail, just like the one Crenshaw talked about. There was one officer in the bunch—a captain."

"Come to think of it, you're right, sir. We were ordered to send out a reconnaissance patrol the day before by that major what's-his-name. You know, the fellow who got under your skin."

"Yeah, I'll never forget him," Pinckney said to the map. "His name was Stairs, claimed he was General Grant's aide-de-camp."

"Tom, I think you should report this to him."

"No, I won't stoop that low."

"But, sir, under the circumstances—"

"Don't worry, Lieutenant, I'll report it alright, but you're going to do it for me." Pinckney shook his head angrily. "No, I'll be damned if I give that man the satisfaction of hearing it from me."

"You're a stubborn man, Colonel."

"You're right, Bernie, I'm stubborn as a mule...but I still have my pride."

It took twenty-four hours for Pinckney's message to climb the chain of command and reach Joshua Stairs at army headquarters in City Point, Virginia.

Initially, he refused to believe Crenshaw's story despite the hard evidence to the contrary. He stared at the initials again and nodded gravely. Yes, the saddlebags belonged to Jon Westmoreland, no doubt about it.

Following a staff conference later that afternoon, Stairs was granted an audience with his boss. Unlike his, Grant's reaction to the news was calmer, businesslike. He showed no trace of emotion when he spoke.

"We knew that sort of thing was possible from the beginning," he said to the half-finished cigar in his hand.

"Yes, sir, only it's too bad. I really thought we had a chance to pull it off."

"Try not to let it bother you, Major."

"But, sir, it was my idea, *my* plan. I'm responsible for what happened." Stairs dropped his chin and stared at the floor. "We lost six good men."

"We've lost many good men in this war, Major, a lot more than I care to think about. Still, Westmoreland knew the risk involved. It was a voluntary assignment."

"But he was a good friend, sir. I'll never allow myself to forget it."

"Perhaps there's a chance the captain *did* survive. After all, his body was never found."

"Yes, sir. But even if he survived, he's bound to be caught sooner or later. If it's happened already, my guess is that he's in Libby prison at this very moment. If that's the case, he'd be better off dead. You know what it's like there."

"Yes, I've read the reports," said Grant gloomily. "On the other hand, what if the Rebs didn't catch him? What if he were able to infiltrate Lee's headquarters and achieve his objective?"

"I think that highly unlikely, General. I'd have received word by now."

"You're referring to the spy at enemy headquarters?"

"Yes, sir. Angel would have sent word by now had Captain Westmoreland succeeded. His information has always been reliable."

Nodding, Grant inhaled through the cigar as he stared at the map hanging from the wall behind them. His eyes soon focused in on a specific spot—Petersburg.

"I'm tired of looking at this place," he said, stabbing it with his index finder. "We've had this town under siege since last summer, and yet the enemy won't budge." A tired sigh. "Actually, you have to admire them for holding out so long."

"Sir, you'll find a way to take Petersburg. When you do, Lee's railway lines will be cut and he'll be forced to surrender. Let's face it, where would he get the food and munitions to supply his army?"

"Lee would find a way," Grant said to the map. "That man always finds a way."

Stairs waited for his boss to turn back before he said, "General, about Captain Westmoreland. Are you going to tell the president what happened?"

"No, I don't think it's necessary. He wasn't very enthusiastic about your plan from the beginning. At least that was my impression. He has enough problems to worry about right now. He's up for reelection, for one thing. More bad news certainly won't help his disposition."

"Yes, sir."

Grant stepped closer and put a comforting hand on Stairs' shoulder.

"I'm sorry about Captain Westmoreland," he said. "He was a fine officer, a credit to the army."

"Sir, I won't rest until I learn the truth of his whereabouts. It will always gnaw at my conscience. I owe it to his wife to find out what happened to him."

"One more thing, Major."

"Sir?"

"About Captain Westmoreland and his mission. Except for him and his men, how many people knew about your plan?"

"Just you, the president and Secretary Stanton."

"What about the spy, did he know?"

"No, sir. I never communicate with Angel directly. He sends messages to me only. I never send any in return for fear he may be found out. It's the best way for him to keep his cover."

"So he never knew about your plan to assassinate Lee?"

"No, sir, not a chance."

Nodding, Grant dropped the cigar to the floor, crushed it to death with his boot, turned and stared at the map again. His eyes and mood seemed distant, and Stairs wondered what was happening in his mind.

"Sir, what are you thinking of?"

"Oh, I was just thinking about Westmoreland again. For instance, let's say he did survive the ambush and wasn't captured. He would still have the element of surprise in his favor. Think of the ramifications if he were able to infiltrate

Lee's headquarters and complete his mission. Maybe the war *would* be over by Christmas. Thus it would save me the trouble of taking Petersburg. Think of the many lives that would be spared."

"You honestly believe it's possible, General?"

"Indeed I do, Major. Captain Westmoreland is a resourceful officer, handpicked for this assignment." A smirk came over the great man's lips. "Let's face it, anything's possible in a war."

At that moment, the idea of assassinating Robert E. Lee was the furthest thing from Jon Westmoreland's mind. Seated at Elsie's table, he was observing the man sitting on the other side who was doing the same to him. For the past hour the rebel officer had been asking him question after question: a polite interrogation. Such bright, piercing blue eyes the man had. An intense soldier who reminded him of another intense soldier—himself. He covered his mouth and coughed.

"Pardon me, Major."

"Quite all right, Colonel," said Wayne Gibson. "Actually, it is I who should apologize. I've asked too many questions, surely. I must be a bore by now. You should rest."

"Yes, I could use it."

"Before I go, just one last question, if you don't mind, Colonel? It's for my report."

"Yes?"

"Well, correct me if I'm wrong, but I recall you saying earlier that it was the Negro who found you after you had been thrown from your horse. Is that right, sir, or did my memory betray me?"

"Everything I told you before is exactly the way it happened."

"Very well." Gibson got to his feet. "You're a lucky man, Colonel Madden. After that incident, and considering how Tombs and his rabble treated you, you're indeed fortunate to be alive."

"Before you leave, Major, I've a question for you."

"Of course."

"How did you know I was here?"

"Why, Sergeant Tombs, of course. You see, Colonel, during his court-martial he confessed to everything that had happened here. In fact, now that I think of it, it's amazing to me how a man with a history of mendacity would suddenly feel remorse and turn honest when facing a hangman's noose."

Nodding, Westmoreland changed the subject.

"Will you be leaving now to return to your regiment, Major?"

"No, my men are exhausted," answered Gibson. "We'll bivouac here tonight and leave first thing in the morning. I'll post a guard outside the door to ensure your privacy." He snapped his heels together. "Colonel."

Westmoreland returned Gibson's salute and watched as the rebel cavalryman turned away and headed for the door. When the door closed behind him, he stood out of the chair and sauntered over to the window, utilizing the cane Elsie had provided.

He peered out and saw soldiers everywhere. Dejected, he

stepped away from the window and sat down on the bed. Strange as it was, he felt safe now despite the fact he was surrounded by the enemy. But they would be gone in the morning, Gibson had assured him. Westmoreland stretched his arms and lay down. Yes, after they were gone tomorrow, he would leave too.

XVIII

Wayne Gibson sat down on the bed roll, stretched his arms and yawned. It had been a long day, and he was dead tired. He stretched again, collecting his thoughts, and dragged the candlestick closer. He opened the journal and read his last entry:

...The disagreeable business of hunting down the outlaws known as the Black Legion is over and done with. Two of the renegades were killed while trying to make their escape. The man called Tombs, having been tried and sentenced, was hanged. In the morning the troop and I will leave this place and rejoin the regiment.

Upon arrival at the plantation this day, I made the acquaintance of a fellow officer, Colonel James Madden, who assured me he is the owner of the place. Although I do not doubt his word, I am puzzled as to his reason for being here. He claims he was invalided out of his regiment due to his battle wounds of several months ago, and yet he seems in fair physical condition despite the fact he wears a head bandage and needs a cane to get around. Both, he contends, were the result of being thrown from his horse.

He has twice refused my offer of medical treatment, insisting he is not fit enough to travel. At present, he's being attended to by a young Negro woman, who is, he claims, a member of his servants. She was the only one of her kind found; the rest having dispersed due to the unique circumstances of the war...

Gibson put the journal aside and scanned the room. Everyone in the parlor was asleep, or so it seemed. As usual, Sergeant Peters snored like a mountain bear in hibernation. He, too, wanted sleep, but the voice inside him told him to wait. He grabbed the candlestick, climbed on his feet and started to explore the mansion, careful not to make noise.

After visiting the kitchen he found the library. It was a large room with plush Oriental carpeting and French doors, the walls lined with row after row of dusty books. Most were law books, he noted, with many published in England over a century earlier. Gibson remained there a while longer, enjoying the place like a youngster let loose in a candy store.

He left the library and started up the winding staircase, using the banister to guide him. He went methodically from room to room, his sharp eye for detail missing nothing. The furniture in each was cloaked in white sheets, with cobwebs and thick pockets of dust seemingly everywhere, growing like mold. The walls were badly in need of a coat of paint, maybe two.

The door to the master bedroom caught his interest. He opened it and probed inside with the candle, spotlighting a large closet at the opposite side of the room. He shuffled closer. It was a woman's closet, filled with a dazzling collection of pink, green, bright yellow, pearl white, and blue party dresses, of which some were embroidered at the hemline with lace in the shape of happy flowers. There was also much evidence where moths had feasted. He wondered who belonged to the lavish wardrobe and what she looked like. No doubt a gay, lovely woman.

A mouse startled him, scampering between his feet and disappearing through a tiny hole in the baseboard. Gibson left the bedroom and returned to the parlor. As he headed for the bed roll, his glance caught the brick fireplace, where a small wood fire was rapidly burning itself out.

He tiptoed across the room, grabbed two pieces of firewood and added them to the flames. The wood flared, blowing heat, and it was then he became aware of the man observing him from the oil painting, which hung crooked just above the mantel. He straightened the picture frame until he was satisfied and saw a thin layer of dust hiding the inscription at the bottom. He wiped away the dust and read, "James Everett Madden, III."

He studied the stern face. The eyes were a determined marble blue, and the hair, cropped short at the sides and combed back across the scalp in neat rows, was the color of beach sand. The man must have been about forty-five years old at the time of the painting, he estimated. Was it a portrait of Colonel Madden's father?

Gibson went back to the bed roll. He blew out the candle and watched the fire, listening to its crackling rhythm clashing with Peters' snoring routine. Like the war effort, the great house was in rapid decay: a hollow dwelling without its owner and the many servants to keep it alive. Would Madden retain ownership of the place after the war, or would the soon-to-be-victorious Yankees deem otherwise?

He thought about Madden again. He wasn't sure why, but there was something peculiar about the man. Yet the name was familiar. He remembered his father telling him about a lawyer from these parts with the same surname who had been a wealthy land owner and served in the state legislature. Was the colonel a son of the middle-aged man in the portrait? And what about the Negro? She was obviously loyal to him, and yet there was something about her that seemed equally strange. Perhaps he would find out more about them in the morning.

Gibson awoke the next day to the sight of Sergeant Lawrence Peters staring down at him. "Lo"—that's what the boys called him—was a homely, broad-shouldered sort who wore a glass eye and a shadow of dark beard to hide the bullet scar he had earned at the Spotsylvania "bloody angle" the previous spring. The veteran sergeant, his crooked smile showing gaps where teeth used to be, leaned down and helped his commanding officer to his feet.

"Thought you was dead, Major," he said, chuckling between words. "Can't never recall you sleeping so late."

"Reckon I was more tired than usual," Gibson told him.

"The boys is saddled and ready to go, sir. And you ain't never gonna believe what happened."

"Believe what, Lo?"

"Well, sir, that darkie made breakfast for all the boys this morning. Thought we'd skip breakfast, like we do most days, but there she was cookin' a mountain of grits and eggs for the boys. Even had cornbread for us. And she's a good cook too, I can tell you for a fact." A broad smile appeared. "You hungry, Major?"

"No, just anxious to leave." Yawning, Gibson donned his cap. "Where's Colonel Madden?"

"Still over yonder in that old shack," was Peters' response. "Said he wasn't feelin' so good."

"I need to see him before we leave."

Nodding, Peters changed the subject.

"Major, do you reckon we can steal that darkie and take her back with us."

"Oh, why?"

"Well, sir, you know what the meals is like back at camp. I'm telling you she can cook up a storm. Ain't never had such a grand meal a'fore." Peters showed that wide country smile again. "What do you say, Wayne? Sure be good for morale."

"Can't do it, Sergeant. Besides, it's a political matter."

"Political matter?" Peters corkscrewed his head, frowning. "Beg pardon, sir, but what the hell you talkin' about?"

"It's simple, Lo. The regimental cook is a personal friend

of mine." Grinning, Gibson winked at Peters, who seemed no more enlightened, and headed for the exit.

Outside, he found his troop of horse soldiers milling around, awaiting his orders to move out, just as Peters had described. A squadron of orioles darted overhead as he made a beeline for the shanty, aware that the morning sun was just moments away from joining the new day. At the door of the hovel, he knocked twice and waited for the obligatory "Come in." When it happened, he took a deep breath, opened the door and walked in. Lying in bed, Westmoreland sat up as the rebel officer brought his boots together and saluted.

"Good morning, Colonel." Gibson turned his attention to Elsie, who was working at the hearth, and tipped his cap. "On behalf of my men, thank you for breakfast, ma'am."

She was caught off guard by his statement, had no idea what to say in return. But then she surprised him when she inclined her head and smiled back, proving to him she appreciated the compliment. He grabbed a chair from the table, positioned it near the bed and sat down.

"My men and I are leaving now, Colonel. I want to thank you again for allowing us to bivouac on your farm. I'd also like to repeat my offer that you indulge in the services of our regimental surgeon. Might be wise to have him look you over."

"No, I'll be fine here, Major. I just need more rest, that's all. I'm sure I'll be back to normal in no time."

"As you wish, sir." Gibson hesitated. "By the way, I couldn't help but notice the portrait in your house."

"Portrait?"

"The oil painting hanging above the fireplace in the parlor. Tell me, sir, is it a portrait of your father?"

This time Westmoreland hesitated. He shot a glance at Elsie for help, and she nodded in return, giving him an answer to use. When he looked back, Gibson was observing him closely.

"Ah, yes, it's my father," he said nervously.

"A handsome man indeed. However, if you don't mind me saying so, you don't seem to favor him much."

"How do you mean?"

"Well, your father has dark brown hair and matching eyes, unlike you, sir."

Westmoreland heard the alarm go off inside him, aware he was on dangerous ground. He shot another glance at Elsie.

At last Gibson heard him say, "You see, Major, it's because I favor my mother's good looks. Everyone used to say so, even my father."

"Of course, I should have thought of that. How stupid of me. My apologies for being curious." Back on his feet, Gibson replaced the chair, turned back and tapped his boot heels together. "I'll be leaving now, Colonel." He saluted as before, completed an about-face, and left the shanty.

Westmoreland stared at Elsie, looking anxious in a desperate sort of way, and she joined him by the bed.

"You look scared, Jon."

"I *am* scared," he said. "I think he suspects something."

Outside, Gibson found Peters waiting for him. The rest of his men were mounted and ready to go. As Gibson approached, Peters sensed something was troubling him. A product of their three years together.

"What is it, Wayne? Looks like you can't make up your mind 'bout somethin'."

"Got an itch that won't go away," Gibson told him. He glanced back at the shanty, scratching his chin thoughtfully, and Peters saw the connection.

"The colonel, sir, is there something wrong with him?"

"Yes, something very wrong, Sergeant. For one thing, he's a liar."

"Sir?"

"Never mind, I'll explain later."

Peters asked, "We leavin' now, Major?"

"No, not yet."

"But, sir, we're due back at camp today."

"Don't worry, we'll get back, but we're going to be late." Gibson clapped him on the shoulder. "Now, Sergeant, here's what I want you to do."

Peters listened as his commanding officer explained what was on his mind. Finished, Gibson headed back toward the mansion. After he was inside, Peters took a deep breath for strength and followed through with his orders.

In the parlor of the great house, Gibson stood by the fireplace and stared at the oil painting above the mantel, his mind racing at top speed. He studied the face of blue eyes, dirty blond hair and jutting chin with more scrutiny. A rich and powerful sort indeed, but obviously no kin to the man in the shanty. Yes, the man in the portrait was the real Colonel Madden, the arrogant slave master and politician his father had told him about.

The door opened behind him. Gibson spun around as Lo Peters entered the parlor, the Negro girl preceding him. Elsie stopped when she saw Gibson, but then picked up her momentum when Peters prompted her with a firm nudge. She was trembling, Gibson noted, with both eyes on the defensive, as if terrified to be in his presence.

A black ghost.

"Good work, Lo. The colonel give you any trouble?"

"No, just wanted to know what I was up to, Major. Told him I was just following orders."

"Very well, you can leave now, Sergeant, I'll handle things from here on. Post a guard outside the shanty. If Madden complains, tell him I'll be with him directly."

"Yes, sir."

When he was gone, Gibson beckoned Elsie with his index finger.

"Come here, girl."

She refused to accommodate him, was still shaking like a scared rabbit. When he beckoned her a second time, she took three steps forward, but no more. Gibson wiggled his finger.

"Come here, I won't hurt you," and she did so with reluctance.

"Yes, sir?"

"It's time we had a chat, don't you think?"

"Don't know what you mean."

"What is your name?" he asked.

No answer. Gibson sighed.

"Look, girl, I don't have a prejudiced bone in my body, which means I've nothing against people of your color.

However, if you don't tell me what I need to know, I might change my mind. You understand me?"

She nodded, and Gibson indicated the oil painting.

"Tell me about this man."

A hush fell over the Willistown hospital as Robert E. Lee walked into the main ward. It was as if a soldier of the Lord had descended upon the place. The wounded inmates, of whom most were injured beyond repair and would not live out the year, sat up in their beds and watched the great man approaching, many suppressing the need to cough. Lee's aide-de-camp, Colonel Taylor, who followed the general into the ward, had witnessed the scene many times before. It never failed to awe him.

Lee stopped at the first soldier's bed and chatted with him briefly before moving on to the next patient. Although he didn't show it, Taylor could sense the general's pain as he went from man to man. His face was the color of ash, his tired eyes bloodshot red. A result, Taylor knew, of the many long days of travel. Yet there was something else. Old age had overtaken the Gray Fox, was showing more so than usual.

Lee made a short speech afterward, thanking everyone for their loyal service. He then expressed his regrets for the sacrifices they had made. "*I* am responsible," he told them. As he turned to leave, one of the patients, a veteran soldier who'd had his left leg amputated at the knee, somehow managed to stand up and shouted after him, "God bless you, General Lee!"

Later that day in a house commandeered for Lee's

personal use, Taylor made mention of the fact that the general appeared overly tired and should rest until he was fit enough to travel. Lee reluctantly agreed and dismissed him. He grabbed his Bible and sat down in the chair next to the fireplace, letting his mind wander.

Yes, Taylor was right. He was certainly unfit to go on. The chest pains were bothering him again, the same which had started after his meeting with the president three days earlier. Lee opened the Bible and started to read, hoping it would settle his nerves.

Following a staff conference later that evening, Lee met with Taylor and Captain William Anderson, one of his top intelligence officers. Anderson's primary job was interrogating high-ranking Union prisoners. His duty that night was to provide Lee with a detailed report regarding the lack of food rations and animal forage needed to sustain the army on a daily basis. The grim news was nothing new to Lee.

"The trains out of Petersburg carry less food all the time," Anderson was saying. "If Grant takes the city before winter sets in, the army will starve."

"We will hold the line at Petersburg!" countered Taylor, his voice close to anger. "Look what we did to Burnside at the Crater. And we will do it again."

"Begging the Colonel's pardon, but that's horse dung," argued Anderson. "Grant can afford the casualties—we can't. The Federals are massing their armies near Ford Stedman, no doubt preparing for a new offensive. We may need to abandon Petersburg long before that happens."

"But that doesn't make sense," Taylor fired back. "You

just said the army will starve if we abandon the city. Which means we're damned if we do, damned if we don't." He noticed Lee staring at him, aware that his outburst was not appreciated. "My apologies, General."

Lee said to him, "I would be grateful, Colonel, if you would please leave now. I wish to have a private word with the captain before I retire tonight."

"Yes, sir." Taylor saluted and withdrew.

Lee said to Anderson, "I want you to be blunt, Captain, and tell me what you're thinking."

"Yes, sir."

"This business at Petersburg does not go well for us, obviously. If we abandon the city, the army would starve. If we don't, it's possible we will succumb to Grant's army in a hopeless battle of attrition. Are you suggesting that I surrender the army at this time?"

"Many lives would be spared, General." Anderson felt a twinge in his left arm, the one that was without its hand. "I regret to say I have no other recommendation at this time."

"If we abandon Petersburg, we will need to give up Richmond as well," said Lee glumly. "If that happens, my staff has recommended that we head south to join General Johnston's army. I must tell you I find the idea distasteful. I could never give up Virginia to those people.

"You've done your duty, Captain. Like you, I wish to end the war as soon as possible, but on a favorable note that is honorable to both Virginia and the president." Lee tendered a short smile. "Please feel free to retire now."

Anderson stepped back and saluted, the bottom three

fingers of his right hand barely touching the bill of his cap. When he was gone, Taylor reappeared.

"Will there be anything else you require this evening, General?"

"I'm not feeling well," Lee told him. "I think we'll stay in Willistown another day or two before returning to headquarters. Please inform General Longstreet of the delay."

"Of course, sir." Taylor hesitated, wondering if the chest pains were bothering his boss again. "General, shall I tell the surgeon to look in on you?"

"No, that won't be necessary," was Lee's answer. "More rest is all I need, I think." He smiled, although it was at best an anemic effort. "Good night, Colonel."

Wayne Gibson marched into the shanty unannounced, his earlier calm exterior having been replaced by an obvious sense of urgency. A man with a singular purpose in mind, observed Westmoreland.

"What is this, Major?"

"My apology for intruding, but a new matter has been brought to my attention."

Westmoreland ignored him.

"Where's Elsie?"

"Interesting you should mention her name."

Westmoreland had no chance to respond as Gibson turned suddenly and marched into the room next door. When he reappeared, he was clutching Westmoreland's uniform. He tossed the clothes on the end of the bed, went back to the door, opened it, and Elsie stepped inside. Her face was grim and glistening with moisture, evidence that she had been doing some crying. Following her was the tobacco-chewing Peters. Gibson cleared the gravel from his throat and spoke to the Yankee.

"Captain Westmoreland, I presume?" To Elsie he said, "Did I get the name right?"

Westmoreland climbed out of the bed.

"My compliments, Major. You're a clever, resourceful man. What now?"

"You're wearing the wrong uniform, Captain. According to the articles of war, that makes you a spy."

"I see. The hangman's noose?"

"Normally that *would* be the case. However, the girl has explained everything to me. Since changing uniforms was not your idea, I'll give you the benefit of the doubt. You see, I'm an educated man who believes in the value of military intelligence."

Gibson dismissed Peters and waited as he left the hovel, Elsie accompanying him. The door closed, and Gibson sat down in the rocking chair, took off his cap, and calmly raked his fingers through his dirty blond hair, as though he had all the time in the world.

Westmoreland heard him say, "I'd be grateful, Captain, if you'd remove the colonel's uniform and slip back into yours. Somehow it just doesn't seem to fit you anymore."

"And after that?"

"Why, isn't it obvious?" Gibson flashed a smirk. "I want to learn more about your mission to assassinate General Lee, of course."

XIX

One of the reasons for the Confederate defeat at Gettysburg was that General J. E. B. Stuart's cavalry did not fulfill its mission. Stuart's goal was to reconnoiter the Federal positions, evaluate their strengths and capabilities, and report back with the information to command headquarters. Because of his blunder, Lee commenced hostilities with very little knowledge of just how dangerous his opponent was.

Strategically, the great battle was decided by concentrated infantry attacks supported by long-range artillery. Cavalry action was limited during the three-day affair, was a minor detail in the overall scheme of things. Although there were isolated clashes between Stuart's Virginians and General George Armstrong Custer's horsemen, most were relatively insignificant hit-and-run skirmishes. It was at Gettysburg when Captain Wayne Gibson had been wounded for the first time.

He was riding point with Sergeant Peters during what seemed to be a routine patrol when the sharpshooter's bullet caught him by surprise, exploding in the meat of his left shoulder. At first it felt like a bee sting. Then, when he saw the blood oozing from between his fingers, he knew that something had to be done, and quick. Fortunately for him, Peters was there to assist.

At the field hospital later that day, Gibson lay on a camp bed waiting for the surgeon to arrive. Having passed out two times already, he thought he was about to go under again when the surgeon finally appeared. The middle-aged doctor apologized for the delay, informed his patient that "we got no laudanum left," and proceeded to extract the bullet, with Gibson watching his every move, a rifle bullet lodged between his teeth.

When it was all over, the doctor showed him the evidence of his pain, offered it to him as a souvenir, and then left to treat the others awaiting his services. Afterwards Gibson slept, thinking his problems were behind him and that he'd be returning to his command in the not-so-distant future. Unbeknownst to him, his problems had just begun.

It started six days later when he awoke to the searing pain in his shoulder. The surgeon was summoned, the same man

who had treated him the first time, and examined the wound.
To his dismay, he found that he had not properly closed the
wound following surgery. In consequence, Gibson's shoulder
had become dangerously infected. The surgeon, a native
Mississippian who'd had an unremarkable practice before the
war, admitted that he had no idea what to use as a quick-
healing remedy. Before proper medical help arrived, the
infection had spread and Gibson lapsed into a coma. The
consensus was that he would die within a week.

The Battle of Gettysburg ended when "Pickett's charge"
was repulsed by Winfield Hancock's valiant Second Corps at
Cemetery Hill. There was a violent rainstorm the following
day as Lee gave the order to retreat. His goal was to cross the
Potomac River and save what was left of his shattered
command. George Meade, the victor of Gettysburg who was
renowned for his cautious style as a battlefield tactician, had
no stomach to pursue the enemy, and Lee's army limped
across the state border unchallenged. Strategically, it was one
of the great blunders of the war by the North.

The wagon train of wounded that followed Lee's army
through Maryland and across the Potomac stretched for
nearly seventeen miles. Many of the wounded died en route
and hundreds more later in hospital. Gibson, who was barely
holding on, eventually ended up in a private Richmond
infirmary.

He was still in coma, had already been issued his last
rights. His father, a member of the state legislature who had
voted against southern secession, learned of his son's
predicament and started pulling strings in an effort to save the

young man's life. After the best medical care was found and administered, it was four days later when his son emerged from coma to the sight of his father smiling above him. By medical standards, his recovery was nothing short of miraculous.

But it would take another two months for his wound to heal, during which congressman and soldier became reacquainted as father and son. Because of his political ties, Nathan Gibson advised his son that it would not be necessary for him to return to combat. "You've done your part in this hopeless struggle." Despite his father's plea that he resign his post and return to private life to pursue a more meaningful, productive life, Wayne was equally stubborn and refused to give in. "I must finish what I started, father. I will *not* abandon my duty."

It was then Nathan Gibson informed his son of his involvement in secret peace negotiations with the Federals, negotiations that would lead, he hoped, to the cessation of hostilities. The news, though stunning at first, did not surprise Wayne. He had known of his father's belief that Virginia's secession from the Union had been a mistake, and that a prolonged war with the Yankees would only lead to ruination of the south. "Diplomacy, not war, is the way for modern civilization to resolve its problems," he remembered his father saying. With the issue of his son's future still uncertain, they parted company. As fate would have it, it was the last time Wayne saw his father, who died of influenza three weeks later.

How very much he had loved his father, yet the differences between them had always stopped them from being close. Wayne put the letter aside, the one he had received informing him of his father's death, the same one he had never had the courage to destroy. Yes, his father had been right. The war had been a hopeless struggle from the beginning. Still, he would not trade a minute of what he had experienced the past three years. When the war was over, then he would pursue a more intellectually fulfilling life, one worthy of his parent's dreams and hopes for him...

Gibson climbed off the stool and threw on his riding blouse. Strange, but he felt tired, and lonely. The business of tracking down the infamous Black Legion had been a dirty job, one he had despised from the beginning. But it had turned out especially profitable, for it had ended in the capture of the Union horse soldier, Jonathan Westmoreland, a West Pointer like himself who had led a heroic detail of sharpshooters in an attempt to bushwhack General Lee and "end the war." Yes, a futile mission from the outset, and yet the whole thing was so fantastic, so exciting.

Lo Peters appeared in the duty tent, disrupting his train of thought. As always the sergeant looked grubby, was badly in need of a wash and shave. Showing at the side of his mouth was that eternal bulge of chewing tobacco. Gibson returned his salute.

"Beg pardon, Major."

"Yes, Sergeant, what is it?"

"Well, sir, Corporal Hodge told me to remind you that you ain't had nothin' to eat all day. He respectfully suggests—"

"I don't need anyone to remind me when I'm hungry," Gibson cut him off. "Anyway, I'm not in the mood." He shuffled the papers on the desk in front of him. "Need to finish my report."

Peters nodded, knowing from experience not to press the issue.

"Very well, sir, it's your stomach. By the way, what are you gonna do 'bout that Yankee captain?"

"I'm not finished with him yet. After that...well, I reckon he'll be sent to Richmond."

"Libby prison?"

"Perhaps."

Peters shook his head and muttered, "A shame, that, sir."

"Oh, how do you mean?"

"Well, considering what happened to him, losing his men that way. Then having to put up with Tombs and his bunch."

"Yes, an extraordinary fellow this Westmoreland."

"Kind of reminds me of you, Wayne," said Peters with a smirk.

"Where is he now, Lo?"

"Still with Doc Clayton. He says you can have him back when he's done with him."

"I can't wait that long. Come on, let's go find him."

At the hospital they found Westmoreland sitting on a camp bed in a small room separating him from the other patients, a sentry standing by the open door. Head down and hands clasped together, Westmoreland was unaware of Gibson watching him.

Since his arrival, the enemy had treated him well. Dr. Jesse Clayton had redressed the head wound and upgraded his condition from critical to satisfactory. The Rebs had even given him a bite to eat. "Fried grits," they had called it.

As Gibson approached, the sentry came to attention and saluted. Westmoreland made an attempt to get on his feet as the cavalryman stepped into the room.

"No need for that," Gibson told him. To Peters he said, "Fetch the surgeon."

Peters withdrew. Gibson grabbed an empty stool nearby, positioned it near the bed and plopped himself down.

"How are you feeling, Captain? Any better?"

"Yes, much better."

"Glad to hear it." Gibson stretched his legs. "I've been working on my report. However, if you don't mind me asking again—"

"I've already told you everything I know, Major. I've nothing more to say."

Just then Peters reappeared, the head surgeon at his side. Gibson got off the stool.

"You wanted to see me, Major?"

Jesse Clayton, a flat-shouldered, fifty-one-year-old man, towered over Gibson by nearly a foot. Wearing a soiled white smock over his uniform, he was a stone-faced sort who always carried with him an unkempt white beard that matched the color of his long curly hair.

Gibson said to him, "I need your opinion of this officer's present condition."

"The captain's head wound is healing fast," said Clayton. "He's a young man. He should live a long life."

"Can he be moved?"

"No, he needs more rest. Perhaps in a day or two."

"Very well, thank you, doctor."

Clayton withdrew, and Westmoreland said, "What now, Major?"

"You heard the man. More rest, then…well, I reckon you'll end up in prison camp for the duration of the war."

"The fate of a captured soldier."

"Of course."

"Actually, I'm obliged to thank you, Major. You've treated me with much respect. Another officer might've reacted differently under the circumstances. Let's face it, I *was* wearing the wrong uniform when you found me. You could've had me shot."

Gibson burst into laughter.

"No, I could never have done that, Captain. I'm not that kind of man, I assure you. But tell me, if you were I, what would you have done? Would you have stood me up in front of a firing squad, thinking I was an enemy spy?"

"No, I suppose not."

"We're a product of our upbringing," Gibson told him. "In fact, you and I are very much alike. We're both proud, educated men, men of high principles who are loyal to their duty, and their country. Take for instance your mission to assassinate General Lee. You said you respected him, and yet you took the job willingly even though the risk was great."

"It was virtually hopeless from the beginning," Jon said to the floor. "Guess I knew that all along."

"The men in your squad, Captain, were all of them *your* men?"

"Yes."

"A pity. I reckon losing them was quite hard on you?"

"As an officer of duty, you already know the answer to that, Major."

"Yes, of course." Gibson stood and put the stool back where he had found it. "Just one more thing before I go, Captain."

"Yes, Major?"

"I need to satisfy my curiosity. Tell me, had you been able to penetrate Lee's headquarters with the opportunity to shoot him, would you have gone through with it?"

"I've asked myself that question many times."

"And what was the answer?"

"I'm not sure. I still don't have an answer."

"Oh, but I think you do, Captain, or you wouldn't be here right now."

"And if the situation were reversed, what would do, Major? Would you shoot General Grant?"

"Oh, but you already know the answer," said Gibson with a smirk. "Indeed you do."

Gibson finished his report and delivered it to his commanding officer; but it did not stop there. A messenger was sent for, and the report quickly climbed the chain of command, eventually making it into the hands of General James Longstreet, commander of the First Corps of the Army of Northern Virginia.

"Fantastic!" was his reaction.

He read the report a second time, then summoned his chief intelligence officer to join him, curious to know his opinion.

"Well, what do you make of it, Major?"

Robert Hazard hesitated. A slight, unassuming man with balding brown hair and hazel eyes, Hazard owned a forgettable, stone-carved face and thick wire-rimmed spectacles that kept the world in front of him constantly in focus. A Richmond detective by trade, he was described by those who knew him as a foul-mouthed, arrogant bastard who could take forever and a day when dissecting a problem that needed on-the-spot resolution. In that regard he and Longstreet had much in common, for the latter was prone to moments of procrastination as well, particularly when confronted with a challenging military problem.

"Hard to say, General," was Hazard's response.

"A plot to assassinate Lee and end the war." Longstreet stroked his beard thoughtfully. "Yes, quite ingenious. One has to wonder why the Yankees didn't try it earlier. Like a year ago."

"Perhaps Lincoln is desperate," suggested Hazard. "Perhaps he felt political pressure to end the war before the election. You've read their newspapers, General. The editorials are highly critical of his war policies, enough to drive any sane man crazy."

"This was a well thought-out plan," said Hazard's superior. "It didn't happen overnight, that's for sure. Must have been approved at the highest level."

"Grant?"

"Yes…or maybe Lincoln himself."

Hazard reread Gibson's report.

"There's something else here, General, something that seems highly coincidental."

"Explain."

"Well, sir, according to Gibson's report, Westmoreland knew exactly where Lee was going to be. In other words, he knew where and when to make the kill. And that kind of information calls for a special brand of intelligence."

"Indeed!" The mood on Longstreet's face was not a pleasant one. "Are you suggesting that there's an enemy spy at army headquarters?"

"Yes, sir, I am," said the ex-detective. "In fact, I'd wager a guess that he's assigned to Lee's personal staff, someone who knows exactly where the general will be at every minute of every day."

"Incredible!" Longstreet said nothing more, and Hazard squirmed noticeably.

"General," he said, "what are you going to do about this?"

"Nothing, the danger to Lee has passed."

"Yes, sir, but what about the spy? Should we not at least investigate this?"

"Exactly what do you propose, Major?"

"Well, sir, we need to root him out."

"And how do we go about that?"

"Well, General Lee is presently staying in Willistown. With your permission, sir, I'd like to go there and bring this matter to the attention of Colonel Taylor. I'm sure he'd want to investigate this, perhaps even consult with Lee's intelligence staff. Let's face it, the spy may want to initiate another attempt on the general's life."

"Very well, Major, you have my authority to proceed. Try to put this matter to rest once and for all. Good luck."

XX

In civilized society the worst thing imaginable is total war: human beings out to destroy fellow human beings. History proves that war has always been man's way of solving his most demanding issues with his neighbor. It is a solution that will probably exist as long as man does.

For the professional soldier, war is the ultimate challenge. It tests his level of intestinal fortitude in wake of what he has learned in the way of battlefield techniques honed by constant training and retraining. For an officer, war measures his ability to lead and motivate others to fight for a common goal. While many are skilled leaders and motivators, the ramifications of war can be a mind-draining experience for others not as gifted, particularly those who experience defeat and dishonor on the battlefield, or lose faith in their duty to continue the fight.

Captain William Franklin Anderson lost his commitment to his duty the day he lost the benefit of the thumb and forefinger of his right hand and the working half of his other limb at the Second Battle of Manassas in August '62. A South Carolinian by birth and honor graduate of The Citadel, Anderson had wanted a military career more than anything else, as early as he had learned to read. He was fascinated with stories of Napoleon's grandiose campaigns and America's victory of independence over Great Britain. "The noble cause of freedom triumphing over tyrannical imprisonment," he had called the latter. When the war for southern independence erupted, he saw a similar cause worth fighting for.

But his fascination with war died on that summer afternoon as he lay unconscious near the creek the Virginians called Bull Run. When he awoke from his coma, he learned that the battle had been another great victory for the South. The Yankees, under the command of Major General John Pope, had been whipped by the invincible Robert E. Lee and hightailed it back to Washington to nurse their wounds. As the Confederacy celebrated, Bill Anderson stewed in a self-made purgatory of anger and remorse. He wished he had died on the battlefield.

His convalescence was slow and painful, during which he reconciled himself to the reality of being a cripple for the remainder of his life. But he was a hero, they told him, and not just another war statistic. In his mind, Anderson was no hero but a cruel result of God's wrath against a society that had gone badly wrong: a half man, half nobody whom historians would write about for future generations to reference in pity and awe. What does a man without an arm, a once proud soldier, do for the rest of his life?

Near the end of his recovery, Anderson befriended his physician, a practicing Baptist minister on the side who also reviled the war and what it was doing to the south, particularly to its most precious resource—its young men. As a result of their bonding, Anderson became "a disciple of the Lord." He "switched" uniforms to serve out the remainder of the war for a new, a more meaningful cause as a soldier in His army. The new enemy was "the devil on earth," his former hero, Robert E. Lee, the man he deemed as the one responsible for what he had become. His new calling was retribution, not only for himself, but the thousands of others like him who had suffered a similar fate.

Refusing to exit the army following his convalescence, Anderson besieged his commanding officer for work suitable for a one-armed invalid. Feeling sorry for him, the major pulled strings and secured an administrative post for him befitting of his education and battlefield experience—military intelligence. As the war dragged on month after bloody month, more able-bodied officers were needed at the front lines, and vacancies abounded within the intelligence corps. By early February '64, Anderson had climbed the administrative chain of command, ending up on Lee's intelligence staff. It was an extraordinary posting which

Anderson described in his diary as an "act of God." He was now an integral part of the devil's inner circle, his chance to smite the wrongdoer at last within reach.

In his new position of authority, Anderson took it upon himself to undermine the cause whenever it suited him without attracting attention. He gave false figures at intelligence briefings and corps staff meetings, issued directives to reroute vital military information to places of war they were least needed. The idea to become a spy for the opposing side happened while he was interrogating a Union officer apprehended at the Battle of New Market in May.

The officer, a cavalryman named Oliver, had been snared by a wandering night patrol. As Anderson discovered, Lieutenant Oliver had been on a mission to relay a priority message from Union headquarters to frontline division commanders. Although the message was of little consequence to the outcome of the battle, Anderson learned that it had originated from a man called Joshua Stairs, a major of rank who was aide-de-camp to Ulysses S. Grant.

The opportunity was too good to pass up. In "the greatest decision of my life," Anderson made a deal with the Yankee and arranged for his escape. On his person, Oliver had the latest ordnance figures in the arsenal of the Army of Northern Virginia. Thus was the beginning of a secret pipeline between Anderson and Stairs, with Oliver the middleman in charge of delivery and Grant the beneficiary of the spy's labor.

Anderson stared at the shorthand scribbling in front of him, the latest entry in his war diary. He shook his head, amazed by his ability to put his thoughts on paper with a hand that had only three usable fingers. He stuffed the diary between two books arranged at the end of the writing desk and remembered he was overdue for a meeting.

He rose from the stool, ignoring the pain in his left arm, which was but a round knob where the elbow used to be, and left to attend the meeting. He arrived in Colonel Taylor's quarters as the meeting was about to commence and apologized for his tardiness. The third man in attendance, the only other one there, surprised him. Taylor opened the meeting.

"Captain Anderson, I believe you know Major Hazard."

"I do, sir." Anderson's blue eyes sparkled like stars as he and Hazard exchanged smiles of friendship. They had served together during the Confederate victory at Fredericksburg in December '62. "Good to see you again, Robert."

"Likewise," chirped Hazard.

Taylor said, "Major Hazard has been dispatched by General Longstreet on a matter of the highest importance." He turned. "Major, if you will?"

"Thank you, sir." Hazard indicated the map table in front of them, cleared his throat and began.

"During the past forty-eight hours we've uncovered a plot to undermine the Confederacy and bring the war to a rapid conclusion. We believe the plot was conceived at the highest level of the Union army." He paused to adjust his spectacles. "To put it bluntly, the plan was designed to rid the army of its most vital asset, our commander-in-chief, General Lee."

"Incredible!" spouted Anderson.

Hazard carried on, "The enemy plan, though brilliantly

conceived, was a simple one: infiltrate our forward lines by stealth and assassinate Lee at a specific place and time. We believe the place was somewhere between army headquarters and Richmond, the time two days prior to the general's meeting with President Davis."

"Extraordinary!" This again from Anderson.

Taylor said to him, "You do realize what this means, of course?"

"Yes, sir, I do. It means the Yankees knew where General Lee would be, either by sheer luck or coincidence, or that they had been given the information beforehand."

"We believe the latter to be the case," Hazard told him.

"But, Robert, that means—"

"That's right, Captain," said Taylor, reading his thoughts. "There's no doubt the Yankees received the information from someone at army headquarters. Which means there's an enemy spy amongst us."

"But, Colonel, that means anyone, including one of us, could be the spy." Anderson shook his head. "How can we be sure he's real?"

"We're very sure," said Hazard. He grabbed the brown envelope on the desk behind him and dropped it on the table. "Here's the proof."

He opened the envelope and extracted several sheets of paper. To Anderson, it looked like an ordinary battlefield action report.

"What is it, Robert?"

"This report was submitted by the commanding officer of the First Virginia Cavalry. They're currently bivouacking at

Hunter's Mill Tavern. The report was composed by a Major Gibson, his most trusted commander. It was Gibson who uncovered the plot and apprehended the would-be assassin." Hazard shoved the report in front of him. "Please read it, Bill. The Colonel and I would like your opinion."

Anderson bowed and began reading Gibson's three-page report. When he was finished, his face was the color of curdled milk.

"This is the most extraordinary thing I've ever read," he said, as if speaking to himself. "It's quite shocking, in fact."

Taylor said, "Imagine if you will, gentlemen, the consequences had this Westmoreland fellow succeeded."

"But he didn't succeed," Hazard reminded him. "However, the matter of the spy still remains. In my opinion, he must be found out and apprehended before he does anymore harm to the army."

"And how do we go about that?" urged Taylor.

"That's why I asked Captain Anderson to join us, sir. He has a sharp mind for this sort of thing. I thought he might be able to help me out."

"Very well." Taylor turned. "Captain?"

Anderson felt the knocking inside his rib cage as he said, "Colonel, the first thing we need to do is have Westmoreland brought here so the major and I can interrogate him."

"But we have Gibson's report," argued Taylor. "Is that really necessary, gentlemen?"

It was Anderson who answered, "Sir, Major Gibson's report is very thorough indeed. However, Westmoreland is the key player in this affair. It's quite possible he knows the spy's name."

"I don't understand," said the bemused Taylor.

"Well, sir, Westmoreland could've been made aware of the spy's identity before he was dispatched on his mission to destroy General Lee. If so, we can pressure him into giving us the spy's name when we interrogate him."

Hazard added, "And the spy *must* be caught—and soon. If he's capable of providing the enemy with information as to where General Lee is at any given time, he's no doubt supplying them with other kinds of information. Perhaps even our battle strategy and troop movements."

"Yes, I see what you mean," said Taylor. "The spy must be rooted out before he exacts any more damage to the army."

"Yes, sir. However, there's one other thing we'll need to do."

"And that is?"

"To conduct the investigation discreetly," was Hazard's reply. "If word leaks out that there's an enemy spy at army headquarters, it could spread like a virus and destroy the troops' morale. Perhaps do even more damage than the spy already has."

"Major Hazard is right," seconded Anderson.

"But what if Westmoreland doesn't talk?" countered Taylor. "What then?"

"Don't worry, Colonel, he'll talk. Believe me, I have many ways of loosening his tongue."

Taylor deliberated, but not for long.

"All right, gentlemen, we'll proceed accordingly." To Hazard he said, "Would it be beneficial for Major Gibson to lend a hand in this?"

"Yes, sir, a good point."

"Very well, Major. Telegraph Hunter's Mill and arrange for Gibson and the Yankee to be sent for immediately. I want this matter put to rest as soon as possible, preferably before the general returns to army headquarters."

The telegraph message addressed to the commander of the First Virginia Cavalry arrived in Hunter's Mill Tavern twenty minutes later. After reading it, he cursed. Still, what could he do? The message was not a request but an order. He had Gibson summoned and explained to him what needed to be done.

Gibson returned to his quarters contemplating his new orders, wondering what it was all about. He dispatched a runner to fetch Sergeant Peters.

"You wanted to see me, Major?"

"Yes, Lo." Gibson was perched on the camp bed, pushing his right foot into his saddle boot. His face was beet red from the effort. "I've just received new orders. I'm leaving for Willistown directly."

"Willistown?" Peters' face clouded. "What for, Wayne?"

"Don't have time to explain, Sergeant, don't know much about it myself."

"Am I going with you, sir?"

"No, you're needed here. I'll take Corporal Hodge with me." Gibson rose from the bed, stomped his boots to get a more comfortable fit, and donned his riding cap. "Is Captain Westmoreland still in the hospital?"

"Yes, sir."

"Is he well enough to ride?"

"I reckon so." Peters squinted. "You takin' him along, Major?"

Gibson nodded and dismissed the hair-scratching Peters. At the hospital, he found Westmoreland where he had last seen him, sitting in the bed. He confronted the sentry at the door.

"Fetch the surgeon, Private."

The soldier left, and Westmoreland said, "I'm surprised to see you again, Major."

"I see you've taken leave of your head bandage, Captain. Feeling better?"

Westmoreland had no chance to respond when the head surgeon appeared in the room, a stethoscope dangling from his neck. He confronted Gibson.

"You wanted to see me, Major?"

"Yes, doctor. Something important's come up, and I'm taking this officer into my charge."

"May I ask on whose authority?"

"Mine."

"Just like that, huh?" The pink-faced physician shook his head. "No, I'm afraid that's not good enough, Major."

"Listen, doctor, I've no time for debate. However, if you'd like to take up the matter with General Lee personally, I'd be obliged to lend a hand."

"General Lee?" The surgeon squinted. "I don't understand."

"The reason is unimportant." Gibson handed over the

telegraph message. "Read this."

The surgeon read.

"Well, I declare...and from Colonel Taylor himself. This *must* be important." He gave back the telegram. "My apologies, Major."

"Never mind that. Now please leave us."

The surgeon obeyed, the door closed, and Westmoreland said, "What was that all about, Major?"

"I've received new orders, Captain. You and I are leaving for Willistown directly." He shrugged. "Why, I don't know."

"So it's not prison camp for me after all."

"No, at least not yet."

"Kind of ironic the way things turned out, eh, Major?"

"How do you mean?"

"Well, I was sent here to kill General Lee in a place I had never even heard of. Now it seems I may have the opportunity to meet the great man in person."

"Yes, but with one exception. Not as an assassin, but as a prisoner of the Confederate States of America."

"Why are you going, Major? What about your duties here?"

"Perhaps General Lee wants to pin a medal on me for capturing the most dangerous man in the Union army."

Gibson had spoken matter-of-factly, without a hint of emotion, and Westmoreland burst into laughter.

"You flatter me, Major, my compliments."

Bill Anderson finished the latest entry in his diary, put the fountain pen aside and read what he had written. Incredible!

A plot to assassinate General Lee and end the war in one bold, lightning-quick stroke. Obviously, the information included in his last message to Stairs, the same which detailed Lee's Richmond itinerary, had been the main ingredient used in the making of the plot. Had it not been for the destruction of the assassin team and capture of its leader, it might have succeeded. Yes, too bad indeed. Still…

There was a knock at the door, ruining his train of thought. Anderson shoved the journal back between the books, conscious of his racing heartbeat.

"Come."

The door creaked open and Corporal Jake Woodley, his orderly, stepped into the room. Woodley was neither tall nor short: a semi-bald, bearded man of thirty-two who had volunteered to serve his country in battle long before the declaration of formal hostilities. The pronounced limp he brought with him—the result of mortar shrapnel at the Antietam "road" two autumns previous—had kept him confined to administrative duties and far away from the front lines. In that regard, he and Anderson had much in common. He saluted.

"Beg pardon, Cap'n."

"Yes, Jake?"

"Was told to tell you that you is required to meet with Colonel Taylor and Major Hazard in the prisoner's hut in five minutes."

Nodding, Anderson grunted as he rose from the stool and reached for his cap.

He heard Woodley say, "Can I help you with somethin',

Cap'n?"

"Yes, Corporal, get my coat."

"A good idea, sir. It's gettin' awfully chilly outside."

It was four minutes later when Anderson arrived at the prisoner's hut. Inside, he found Hazard and Taylor waiting for him. There were two other officers in attendance, both young men but wearing different uniforms. The man in Confederate gray was a head size shorter than the one in Yankee blue. Anderson felt the lightning bolt rush through him.

"Thanks for coming, Bill," Hazard said to him, smiling. He indicated the new arrivals. "I believe you know why these gentlemen are here."

"Yes, sir." Anderson faced Taylor. "Colonel, with your permission?"

"By all means."

"Thank you." Anderson stepped up to Gibson and brought his boots together. "A privilege to meet you, Major. My name is Anderson." They exchanged salutes. "They tell me you should have died at Gettysburg, sir."

"'Fraid I shall never die, Captain," said Gibson with a smirk.

Anderson turned. "So you're the notorious Captain Westmoreland?"

A rhetorical question, but Westmoreland answered nevertheless with a curt nod. Anderson made an about-face and rejoined Taylor and Hazard.

Taylor said to him, "These officers have ridden a long way and need rest. You and the major will begin work first thing in the morning."

"Yes, sir."

"Very well." Taylor turned away and headed for the exit, Anderson a step behind him.

The door closed, and Hazard said to Gibson, "I regret to say that we don't have separate quarters for you and the captain. You'll both have to stay here tonight. I'll have sentries posted outside the door. Do you want the prisoner handcuffed, Major?"

"No, that won't be necessary," Gibson told him.

Westmoreland said, "Major Hazard, you've still not told me why I was brought here."

"That will be explained to you in the morning, Captain." Hazard donned his cap. "Until tomorrow, gentlemen."

XXI

He saw the holster in the dim light but not its contents. Sitting on a stool next to the camp bed, the gun belt was eight, maybe nine steps away, less if he was quick about it. He observed his rival's prostrate form. Lying on his side, face to the wall, Gibson had not moved in the past quarter hour. But was he asleep? Westmoreland thought, weighing his options. Even if he were able to reach the gun, then what?

He crawled out of the bed without a sound, was across the room like a cat and clawing at the holster flap before he had time to change his mind. No reason to be silent now, he yanked out the Colt revolver, cocked the hammer, and saw Gibson stir. When the cavalryman rolled over and opened his eyes, he was staring down the barrel of his gun.

"A good try, Captain." Gibson rubbed the sleep from his eyes, sat up and stretched his arms. "Reckon I'd have done the same thing."

Westmoreland released the hammer of the empty Colt and tossed it on the end of the bed.

"I had to try, Major, but you knew that, or the gun would have been loaded."

"Of course. I'd have been disappointed had you *not* tried." Gibson reclaimed the revolver and put it back where it belonged. "Like I said before, we're two of a kind. A pity we're on opposite sides."

Westmoreland waited as the Virginian dressed himself before he said, "What's going to happen today?"

"Well, I reckon you'll be interrogated by Major Hazard and the other fellow we met last night." Gibson struck a match and lit the oil lamp hanging from the ceiling, adding more light to the room. "Odd, but I've forgotten his name already."

"Anderson."

"Ah yes, Anderson." Gibson pursed his lips. "The man with one arm is a strange one."

"How do you mean?"

"It's hard to explain, but there's something about him that makes me nervous. He seems an embittered man, someone who wears a chip on his shoulder. For some reason I don't trust him."

"Intuition, Major?"

"Perhaps."

"He lost an arm in combat," Jon reminded him. "I'd say he has a right to be bitter."

"True, but like you and me, Anderson is a soldier. He knew the risk involved when he put on the uniform."

"You state the obvious, Major. Tell me, what really bothers you about him?"

"Something in his voice, I reckon. It's as though he were happy to be here. His reaction toward you was particularly interesting…like you were a lab specimen to study."

There was a knock on the door, startling them. Gibson opened it and shivered as a burst of crisp morning air smacked him in the face.

"Yes, Corporal?" he said to the young soldier standing there.

"Major Hazard sends his compliments, sir. Wants to know if you'll join him for breakfast." He indicated the mess tent at the other side of the road. "Over yonder."

"Tell the major I'll join him directly."

The soldier saluted and left at the double quick. Gibson grabbed his jacket from the coatrack and draped it over his shoulders, then reached for his gun belt and wrapped it around him.

Westmoreland heard from him, "I'll make sure you get something to eat, Captain," and the door closed behind him.

It was spitting rain, a dreary, wind-swept dawn. Steel-gray storm clouds were out in abundance, shielding Willistown from the warmth of the new day's sunlight.

Gibson stopped at the entrance of the mess tent and saw several campfires aglow in the encampment on the outskirts of the village, soldiers milling around them like picnic ants. Other than that, there was very little activity.

To his far left was a church steeple towering above a wall of maple trees, their naked limbs glistening in the morning mist. On his far right and directly across from the hospital was a row of tall white houses stretched along the street, most seemingly in disrepair, with three sentries posted outside the one nearest him. No doubt where Lee and his staff were billeted, he concluded. The wind gusted, scattering leaves and other debris across the road. Gibson shook the rain from his cap and walked in.

The place was big enough to feed a dozen people. He counted four officers in attendance. Three were seated together and eating. The fourth was Robert Hazard, the man he had met the previous evening. Hazard was sitting by himself two tables away from the others, an empty plate in front of him. Gibson joined him.

"Good morning, Major Hazard."

"Ah, good of you to come," said Hazard cheerfully. He indicated the chair opposite, and Gibson sat down, making himself comfortable.

"Coffee smells mighty tempting," he said.

"Yes, a rare thing these days." Hazard filled Gibson's coffee cup. "Sorry, but we don't have any milk or cream, just sugar."

Gibson took the sugar bowl from him and flashed a grin.

"Much obliged."

"Looks like we're in for another dose of rain today," said Hazard, watching as Gibson sank a teaspoon of sugar into the cup. "Seems like that's all we get these days."

"It'll keep the Yankees on their side of the picket line."

"A good point." Hazard waited as Gibson sampled his coffee, then said to him, "We've an important visitor in Willistown today. Any idea who it is?"

"No," lied Gibson.

"General Lee." Hazard sipped from his cup and continued, "I was told he's been here since yesterday. Colonel Taylor informs me that he's not in the best of health. Chest pains of some kind."

Gibson made no effort to respond, had nothing worthwhile to contribute. Hazard cleared his throat.

"You're no doubt wondering why we're making such a bother over this assassination business." Hazard's words were spoken in a soft tone, were audible only to them. "However, I can tell you that it's crucial to the war effort that we find the spy and make him talk."

"Spy?"

"Yes. From the report you submitted, I came to the conclusion that the Yankees couldn't have known of General Lee's whereabouts unless they had been given the information beforehand. I believe the enemy has an agent working undercover at army headquarters."

"Indeed!"

Hazard continued, "We must know the full extent of the spy's activities. We must know what kind of information he's been feeding the enemy, how he's doing it, and so forth."

"Westmoreland made no mention of a spy when I interrogated him," Gibson told him. "Anyway, I doubt he'd know."

"But what if he *does* know?"

"No, I think that's unlikely, Major. What I mean is, why would his superiors send him on a mission with that kind of information? If he were captured and revealed the spy's name, it would compromise his position and he'd be useless to them." Gibson shook his head. "No, it doesn't make sense to me. I don't think he knows the spy's name."

"Still, we must try to find out. We've no other recourse. In fact, maybe you can help."

"Oh, how?"

"When you're alone with him, try to find out as much information as you can. He may be more open with you, more comfortable in your company, so to speak."

"Captain Westmoreland is a dedicated officer of duty, sir. If he knows the spy's identity, he surely won't tell me. No, I'd only be wasting my time."

An awkward pause followed before Hazard changed the subject.

"Tell me, Major Gibson, what's your opinion of the war? Do you think we still have a chance to win?"

"If you believe that, you'll believe anything." There was no reaction from his peer, and Gibson carried on, "We lost the war when Sherman captured Atlanta. The south has been cut in two, sir, and food stores have evaporated to almost nothing." He held up his cup. "For example, no milk for our coffee. That must tell you something."

"What about a negotiated peace?"

"That's already been tried."

"By your father and others, for instance?"

"Oh?" Gibson fondled the stubble under his chin, eyes fixed on the man staring back. "You seem well informed, Major Hazard. Who told you that?"

"My job is intelligence, sir. It's no secret to President Davis and trusted members of his cabinet that several congressmen, including your late father, were involved in secret peace talks with their counterparts in Washington."

"My father told me very little about it," Gibson said to his cup.

"But he did tell you why the negotiations failed?"

"Yes, he did. He said Lincoln was adamant and refused to hear our plea for sovereignty."

"So we fight on with no chance of victory. Tell me, Major, as a career officer, how do you feel about that?"

"My job is to serve my country as a soldier, whether in victory or defeat," Gibson told him. "I'm committed to my duty."

"But as the son of a congressman, you do have an opinion?"

"I believe I've already expressed that, sir. The war is lost. It's time we made terms with the Yankees. Too many lives have been sacrificed for a cause that has little meaning now."

"So what you're telling me is that General Lee should be held accountable for allowing the senseless slaughter to continue."

"General Lee is a soldier, just a soldier," Gibson reminded him. "He takes his orders directly from the president. It's Jeff Davis who will be held accountable for the conduct of the war. *He* will bear the burden of responsibility when it's over, not Lee."

"An interesting viewpoint. You sound like a diplomat, Major. Tell me, what are your plans after the war? Do you intend to run for state congress, like your father?"

"I've thought about it," Gibson said to his cup. "There will be much work to do when the war is over. Virginia, like the rest of the south, will enter a difficult period of reconstruction. To serve as a congressman and help the state back on her feet would be a noble undertaking for anyone. But whether I do or not, Virginia will survive and flourish again. She will rise from the ashes of this war—like the phoenix."

"Well spoken, Major. You're an optimist in the face of adversity, the kind of man we'll need when the war is over."

"Now *you're* beginning to sound like a diplomat, sir."

Just then a mess orderly appeared at their table holding a tray of hot food. He served Hazard first, filling his plate with a small slice of fried ham and grits. Gibson was given a similar portion.

The orderly withdrew, and Gibson said, "What about Captain Westmoreland? He'll be fed, of course?"

"I've already given the order," Hazard told him. "We believe he'll talk more freely with a full stomach." He made a wide smirk. "Don't you agree?"

"Sure, if you believe pigs can fly."

*   *   *

"You're being most unreasonable, Captain. Perhaps you're too tense." The rock-faced interrogator reached under the desk, produced a small box and opened it. "Would you like a cigar?"

The prisoner shook his head.

"The interrogation is routine procedure," continued Hazard. "Please cooperate, it's quite painless, I assure you."

"I've already told you everything I know, Major."

Hazard sighed. He glanced at the fidgety Anderson, who was seated next to him on his left. Standing at a window behind the prisoner was Gibson. Arms folded together, the cavalryman was observing the proceedings with religious interest, missing nothing that was being said. Hazard studied the prisoner. To him, Westmoreland seemed unflustered by what was happening, would surely be a tough nut to crack. Yes, a soldier of discipline, just as Gibson had mentioned at breakfast. No doubt a product of his West Point training. The interrogator adjusted his spectacles and continued.

"Tell me, Captain," he said, "what did Grant hope to gain by killing General Lee?"

No answer.

"Well?"

"I've already explained that to you," Jon told him.

"No, you've told me nothing of value," argued Hazard. "Now tell me, what was the reason?"

"My job was to kill Lee, nothing more. He was a military target, just like any ordinary soldier."

"General Lee is hardly an ordinary soldier," Hazard

corrected him. "The Union High Command must've had a higher motive other than to kill Lee just for the sake of killing him. What was it, Captain? To destroy our morale, hoping his death would force the Confederacy to seek a negotiated peace?"

"Why would we want that, Major? We're winning the war, or hadn't you noticed?"

Anderson interjected, "If you think your side is winning, then why try to assassinate Lee? What was Lincoln's motive?"

"Lincoln!" Westmoreland corkscrewed his head in a show of bewilderment. "What's *he* got to do with it?"

"The order to assassinate General Lee had to have come from the highest level of your government," said Hazard. "You mentioned that before. It's in Major Gibson's report."

"I gave him no such information."

All eyes turned as Gibson said, "It was the Negro who told me that, Major. It was she who implicated Lincoln and Grant as the chief architects in the plot to assassinate the general. Obviously, the captain had confided that in her before I was able to determine—"

"Yes, we know all about that," said Anderson, cutting him off. He faced the prisoner. "Now, Captain, it's time to separate fact from fiction. You were captured wearing the uniform of a Southern officer. If we choose, you could be hanged for espionage."

"That was not his doing!" thundered Gibson. "I would suggest that you read my report again, Anderson. You'll note it was the Negro who switched uniforms. It was a matter of the captain's survival."

"We're to trust the word of a darkie?" Anderson laughed without mirth. "Come now, Major, be sensible. Perhaps it's the fairy tale he wanted you to hear."

Hazard said, "Bill Anderson has brought up an interesting point. Perhaps the captain's mission was to infiltrate Lee's headquarters by masquerading as this Madden fellow. Let's face it, he would've had a much better chance of completing his mission."

"No, I don't believe that," countered Gibson. "Besides, how do you explain the ambush of his detail? Do you honestly believe he just walked away while his men were being slaughtered and changed uniforms to infiltrate Lee's headquarters and kill him?" He punctuated his words with a sarcastic chuckle, inciting an immediate reaction from Anderson.

"I take exception to your facetious attitude, Major. It's almost as if you're trying to protect the Yankee."

"Jon Westmoreland and I share a common heritage, Captain. We're both West Point alumni. And that means he deserves fair treatment from all of us. It's in the military code of conduct. It's my intention that he be given an honorable hearing, and nothing less."

"You're not in charge of this hearing!" Anderson corrected him. "Major Hazard is!"

Hazard said, "Gentlemen, please, this is getting us nowhere in a hurry." To Westmoreland he said, "Please be assured, Captain, that you will receive fair treatment befitting of your rank in the United States Army. However, I do require specific information in return." He said to Anderson,

"Proceed."

Anderson took a deep breath and said to the prisoner, "Now, shall we cut through the horse crap and get to the heart of the matter? Did you or did you not change uniforms in an attempt to infiltrate army headquarters and assassinate General Lee?"

"No."

"Then please tell us why you were apprehended wearing the uniform of a Southern officer. Did your own magically change colors?"

"I've already explained that in my report!" shouted Gibson.

"I was talking to the prisoner!" hollered back the one-armed man. He glared at the prisoner. "Well, Captain?"

"The colored girl saved my life," Westmoreland told him. "She switched uniforms while I was unconscious because mine was damp with rain. She was afraid I'd catch pneumonia. But the idea of infiltrating Lee's headquarters as a Confederate officer never crossed my mind, even when the opportunity seemed feasible. As far as I'm concerned, my mission ended when my men were killed."

Anderson was beside himself.

He said to Hazard, "Sir, are we to accept this officer's outrageous deposition? With all due respect to Major Gibson, I find it laughable, an insult to our intelligence."

Hazard said to the prisoner, "The fact remains, Captain, that you were captured wearing the wrong uniform. If I choose to disbelieve your story, you could be tried for espionage and hanged. We have that right under the articles of war." To Anderson he said, "We're wasting time, Bill, get on with it."

Anderson took another deep breath and said when he exhaled, "We're still waiting for the right answer, Captain. If we don't get it, you'll be wearing a hangman's noose in the morning."

"I've already given you the right answer, Captain Anderson. I've nothing more to say."

Hazard said to the prisoner, "Because you were wearing Colonel Madden's uniform when you were captured, I've no alternative but to charge you with espionage. However, if you cooperate by telling me what I need to know, I promise you'll live to see another day."

"But I've told you everything, Major."

"On the contrary, there is one more thing you can tell me. If you cooperate, you'll be spared the dishonor of execution." Hazard removed his spectacles and cleaned them with a kerchief. "Tell him, Bill."

Anderson stood and glared at the Yankee, his eyes bayonets.

"Captain, in order for your mission to succeed, you had to be informed of General Lee's whereabouts before lighting out on your adventure to murder him. We believe the information originated from General Lee's headquarters."

Westmoreland erupted into a volcano of laughter.

"Exactly what are you trying to say, Captain Anderson? Are you telling me there's a spy at Lee's headquarters and that I know his name?" More laughter. "Sorry, but I don't."

"Think harder, Captain. Remember, you save yourself if

you provide us with the right answer."

"But I told you, I don't know his name!"

Anderson was livid, seemed on the edge of losing his nerves. Watching him, Hazard decided it was time for him to regain control of the proceedings.

He said to the prisoner, "Are you married, Captain?"

"Yes, what of it?"

"Well, I was thinking that after the war you'd want to see your wife again."

"Naturally, I'd like nothing better than…"

Silence entered the room.

Hazard waited for the Yankee to finish, but Westmoreland did not oblige him. His dander was up. He knew exactly what the interrogator was hoping to accomplish by bringing his wife into the debate. Gibson also knew it.

He marched away from the window with alacrity and confronted the ex-policeman. The mask on his face was that of contempt, like his voice when he spoke.

"Major Hazard, your attempt to use the captain's wife to provoke an answer from him is without scruples, most unbecoming of your rank. As a fellow officer, I strongly protest."

"This is war!" Hazard reminded him. "At this point I'll do anything to get the information I need."

Westmoreland said, "Major Gibson is right, sir. Bringing my wife into this will do you no good."

"I'll be the judge of that!" Hazard fired back.

"But I've told you everything I know. How many times do you need to hear it?"

"You're lying!" The shouted words belonged to Anderson.

Hazard appeared not to have heard him; his eyes were locked with Westmoreland's.

"His name, Captain, or I can't be responsible for what happens to you. Your fate will rest in the hands of a military court."

More silence.

"Well?" Hazard's question was a demand, not a request.

"I don't know the spy's name," Jon told him.

"So you finally admit there *is* one." Hazard pursed his lips. "What is his name?"

"I don't know—and that's the truth."

"Come now, Captain, his name."

"But I told you, I don't know his name. All I know…"

"Yes?"

"I…only know his cover name."

"Cover name! What cover name? What are you talking about?"

Again no response.

"Well, Captain, I'm waiting."

"I can't remember."

Hazard's eyes flared.

"You're beginning to try my patience, Captain. Now, for the last time, what is his cover name?"

Westmoreland licked dry lips as he tried to remember what Joshua Stairs had told him. Finally it came to him.

"His cover name is…"

"Go on."

"He's called 'Angel'," Jon said to the folded hands on his

lap. He looked back. "That's all I know—I swear!"

"He's lying!" cried Anderson, but again Hazard was not listening.

He said to Westmoreland, "Thank you for your cooperation. That's all for now." Hazard beckoned the sentry standing by the door. "The corporal will escort you back to your quarters."

When they were gone, Gibson confronted Hazard again. His face was not happy, his words even more so.

"Sir, I strongly protest at the way the prisoner is being treated."

"Sorry, Major, but the matter is out of your hands. Leave the business of interrogation to those who are trained to do it." Hazard lit a cigar. "Is there anything else?"

"No, I've heard quite enough."

XXII

The tall, grim-faced man stood ramrod straight on the wooden platform as the harsh dawn wind lashed against him. Hands tied behind him and the rope locked around his neck assured the spectators that there was no place for him to go. Then, suddenly, there was a shouted command, the trap door was sprung, a gasp from the crowd, a screaming *"No!"* from the lone female in attendance, and the blue-clad soldier plunged into the blackness of no return...

Jon Westmoreland opened his eyes and cursed, something he rarely did. His body trembled, and his skin was damp with perspiration as he tried to forget the nightmare. But he failed, just as he'd failed the time before, and the time before that. He could still feel the wind's bite, the scratchy noose; could still see the gray soldiers staring up at him with contempt in their eyes as they awaited the inevitable; and he could still hear the echo of his sobbing wife speaking heavenwards, beseeching the Almighty to intervene and spare his life…

Wayne Gibson appeared at the door, startling him. He marched into the room as if behind schedule, shut the door, and their eyes locked. The rebel horse soldier then turned away, removed himself of his wet poncho and cap, and hung them on the hook behind the door. Turning back, he grabbed an empty stool from the corner, placed it near the bunk and sat down. By then, Westmoreland was sitting upright in the bed, both feet on the cold floor. He wore a long face and was clutching his abdomen like a mother cradling her newborn. Gibson thought he looked abnormally pale, older.

"Well, Major, you have news for me?"

"Yes." Gibson shook his head gloomily. "I regret to say, not good news."

The trap door was sprung, a gasp from the crowd…

Gibson went on, "I saw Colonel Taylor and complained on your behalf, but he told me there was nothing he could do. Said Hazard had complete authority in the matter."

"I never thought it would end like this," Jon said to the floor. "I wish now I had died with my men."

Gibson hesitated briefly before he said, "Didn't know you were married, Captain. I'm sorry."

"I wasn't married that long, not even a month."

"I see." Gibson got off the stool. "Is there anything you'd

like to tell me before I leave?"

"No, Major—and that's God's truth."

Nodding, Gibson replaced the stool, lumbered over to the coatrack and redressed himself with poncho and cap. He glanced back at the Yankee cavalryman, looking as if wanting to say more, but no words came out from between his lips. He reached for the door handle and let himself out.

Westmoreland climbed off the bunk and made his way over to the window, drew the curtains and peered out. There were two soldiers in dark coats standing guard nearby, heads together in conversation. A horse-drawn wagon passed in front of him, accompanied by four Johnny Rebs on horseback. He reached up to close the curtains, but stopped when he saw Gibson standing outside the big house at the opposite side of the road, addressing the sentry at the door. A moment later the sentry saluted, opened the door, and Gibson stepped inside.

The trap door was sprung, a gasp from the crowd…

Jon Westmoreland cursed again, this time with more feeling, shut the curtains and returned to the bunk, clutching his stomach.

"Sir, I object to the way Captain Westmoreland is being treated."

Gibson was standing opposite Hazard, who was seated at the writing desk with pencil in hand, a collection of papers in front of him.

"Sorry, Major, but there's nothing I can do about it."

"But it's inexcusable," said Gibson. "If I must, I'll go to

General Lee and ask him to intervene."

"What makes you think he would?"

"Because he's an honorable man."

Hazard adjusted his spectacles as he studied the intensity in his peer's bright blue eyes. Yes, Gibson was an incorrigible sort, no doubt one used to getting his way. Hazard indicated the empty chair at the side of the desk.

"Please sit down, Major."

Gibson sat.

"I admire your concern for the Yankee prisoner," said Hazard. "This brotherhood between West Point alumni is quite unique indeed. I honestly wish I could help, sir, but I've a job to do here. Surely you can respect that."

"Sir, you came here with the sole purpose of tracking down the enemy spy. But how can you be sure he exists?"

"Oh, he exists, rest assured. There's no other logical deduction. Besides, Westmoreland confirmed it. You heard him, you were there."

"But why threaten him with execution? What good would come of it?"

"Because it's the best, the fastest way to make him talk," replied Hazard. "We need to know who the spy is. More importantly, we need to know how he goes about supplying the enemy with information."

"And when you find him, then what?"

"Well, normally spies are hanged when they're found out. However, in this particular case, I've something else in mind."

"Explain."

"The possibilities are endless, Major. If we determine who

the spy is without him knowing about it, we can use him to our advantage. We can feed him information that *we* want him to know, meaning the enemy will get useless information from him."

"In other words, let him continue to operate, only this time with information supplied by you?"

"Precisely."

"Ingenious, but how does that win the war?"

"Only time would answer that," said the interrogator. "And that's why we must keep the pressure on Westmoreland. Time is running out."

"But what if he *is* telling the truth? What if he doesn't know the spy's name?"

"But he's already given us a lead—a cover name. My plan is to let him stew for a while, and perhaps later he'll talk more freely. Most men do, knowing if they don't, they'll be facing death in the morning."

"But blackmailing a man with his own life is beyond reason," argued Gibson. "Jon Westmoreland is a soldier of duty...and integrity. He deserves better treatment from us."

"Agreed. But in my line of work, I must make some very unpleasant decisions at times. At this stage of the war, I will stop at nothing short of killing a man in order to help the war effort. If you don't agree with that, then perhaps you're in the wrong profession."

"Yes." Gibson rose from the chair. "Perhaps you're right."

Gibson did not give up. He revisited Taylor, hoping he would rescind his decision not to encroach upon Hazard's authority, but the Colonel was stubborn and refused to give in. Gibson then requested an audience with Lee to plead his case, but "the general is too busy and cannot be disturbed," was Taylor's rejoinder.

Dejected, Gibson returned to the prisoner's hut. To his surprise, the sentry was not there. When he opened the door and peeked inside, neither was Westmoreland. An explanation was in order.

"The prisoner was taken to the hospital a short while ago," Hazard told him.

"What happened?"

"He was complaining of stomach cramps. I was told by the doctor that he vomited several times on the way to the hospital."

Gibson smirked at Hazard.

"Well, sir, it appears that your psychology is working at last." Gibson's words were spiked with a sarcastic edge. "You must be proud of yourself."

"I've done my duty, Major—I'm proud of that. But don't look down your nose at me, sir. I'm sure you've made many decisions in your military career you're not proud of."

"Yes, I've made mistakes. And I'll make many more before my time's up on this godforsaken earth."

Gibson wanted to say more, but kept his head and abandoned the urge of telling Hazard why his stomach churned and blood boiled; why he was but a heartbeat away from venting the anger and frustration eating away inside him ever since yesterday's debacle of an interrogation; and why he disapproved of the man's unscrupulous tactics that ridiculed an honorable, fighting soldier. No, he wouldn't tell Hazard what he was thinking, for he knew he'd only be wasting his time.

As he turned away and headed for the exit, Hazard called after him, "Before you leave, Major, I've some important news for you."

"Yes?"

"I was informed a while ago that General Lee and his staff will be leaving Willistown in the morning. I was also told that you, sir, will be leaving tomorrow."

"Oh?"

"You've been ordered to report back to Hunter's Mill and rejoin your regiment." Hazard held up a slip of paper. "Your new orders, signed by Colonel Taylor."

"What about my prisoner?"

"Captain Westmoreland is no longer in your charge."

Gibson walked back to the desk and was given the document. When he had finished reading, he said, "Well, it would seem I've no say in the matter."

"No, Major, I'm afraid you don't."

The spy with the cover name of "Angel" removed his cap and sat down at the writing desk. The three fingers of his right hand ached as he reached between the books to retrieve his war journal. He read his last entry, studying his scribbling as though it were sacred script, and grabbed a pencil. Would this be his final entry?

He thought about what he would do. Perhaps it was time for him to make his escape before Westmoreland exposed him. No, no one knew his true identity or the dangerous game he was playing. Not even Joshua Stairs, to whom he had been supplying key military information for the past four months, knew his real name. Yes, for the time being he was safe.

He scratched out a short paragraph, reviewed what he had written, and replaced the journal. He grunted as he struggled to stand and glanced around the room, searching for his coat. He found it hanging from the hook behind the door, exactly where Woodley had left it before leaving for supper. He stepped across the room and reached inside the right-hand pocket.

He removed the derringer, holding it carefully. It was loaded, both barrels, he saw. Bill Anderson inhaled nervously and replaced the handgun.

The hospital was a large facility, dim-lit, gloomy, the perpetual noise of wounded men permeating the air. Gibson was greeted at the door by a mustached, middle-aged man wearing a soiled white smock. He explained why he was there and was escorted to a private room away from the main ward. The sentry standing guard by the door stiffened at the sight of the cavalryman approaching. Gibson ignored him and opened the door.

Inside, he found Westmoreland lying on a camp bed, eyes closed as if in sleep. Gibson stepped closer and cleared his throat, rousing him. Westmoreland sat up.

"How are you feeling, Captain?"

"Better, but I'm still weak."

"You've been through a lot," said Gibson needlessly. "All

you need is more rest."

"Perhaps."

Gibson went on, "I'll be leaving in the morning, Captain." A pause before he added, "Strange how our paths crossed the other day. But that's war, I reckon."

"Yes."

"And for what it's worth, I'm sorry."

"I understand, Major."

Gibson turned to leave, but was forced to stop when Westmoreland reached out and grabbed his arm.

"One more thing, Wayne. Whatever happens, good luck to you. I know that sounds strange considering we're on opposing sides, but I truly mean it."

"Yes, Jon, I believe you do."

They shook hands, and then Gibson left the hospital.

XXIII

Robert E. Lee raised his chin and made a face of pain as he confronted the three men standing opposite him at the map table.

"Well, gentlemen, there it is—the latest situation report out of Petersburg." Lee gripped the edge of the table with both hands, as if he would fall down if he let go. Taylor, flanked by the others, Hazard and Anderson, thought his boss seemed abnormally tired. "As you can see, it's not good news," he added.

Taylor said, "Sir, would it not be better if you stayed off your feet for a while?"

"No, Colonel, I'll be fine."

Anderson said, "General, with your permission?"

Lee inclined his head, giving Anderson the floor.

"General, sir, the supply trains out of Petersburg are inadequate. The army needs more food and munitions."

"We'll just need to make more sacrifices," said Taylor. "Tighten our belts another notch."

"But for how long?" countered the invalid.

"We've managed with these privations before," Lee told him. "Since the president is unable to supply me with more provisions, we'll have to make do with what we have. I know that's hard to swallow, but there it is."

"Yes, sir." Anderson dropped his chin. "I beg your pardon."

Lee said to Hazard, "You will remain in Willistown tomorrow to clear up this spy business?"

"Yes, sir."

"Very well."

"General Lee?" Anderson again.

"Yes, Captain?"

"Sir, with your permission, I'd like to stay here another day and help the major with the interrogation of the enemy prisoner."

"No, I cannot honor that request. Your services are needed at army headquarters." Lee turned, facing his aide-de-camp. "Colonel Taylor, I wish to have a private word with you before I retire this evening."

"Of course, sir." Taylor dismissed the others. "General?"

"I honestly don't believe that there's a spy at headquarters," Lee told him. "The idea is too preposterous."

"Major Hazard is convinced, sir. The Union High Command *did* try to assassinate you."

"That, too, I find difficult to believe. Why would General Grant risk the lives of six men to snuff out the life of one soldier? Even if they'd succeeded, the president would only have replaced me with someone else."

"But, sir, that's exactly why Grant ordered the attempt on your life. He knows that we could never replace you. You're the one man holding the army together."

"Perhaps it is God's will that I've survived this long. I can think of nowhere I'd rather be than here, with the army."

"General, you need rest. Tomorrow we start early in the morning. We've a long ride ahead of us"

"You're right," said Lee. "Just one other thing before you go."

"Sir?"

"Tomorrow is Sunday. Do you think the chapel minister would agree to perform a private service on my behalf before we leave? Perhaps before reveille?"

"Of course, sir." Taylor nodded. "I'll arrange it."

Taylor had little appetite and skipped supper that evening. Later, he summoned Hazard and Anderson to his quarters to get an update on the prisoner interrogation. Lee's adjutant was neither surprised nor pleased when he was told of their lack of progress.

"So the spy's identity remains a mystery."

"The only thing we've learned so far is the spy's cover name," said Hazard. "'Angel', the Yankee called him."

"Which means absolutely nothing."

Hazard went on, "Colonel, Westmoreland is close to the breaking point. If we keep the pressure on him, I'm certain he'll eventually tell us the spy's name."

"Agreed," chirped Anderson.

"I beg to differ with you, gentlemen," said Taylor. "Anyway, we don't have the benefit of extra time. This Yankee is a tough nut to crack. Major Gibson was right. I doubt Westmoreland knows the spy's name."

"But, Colonel, we *must* keep trying," said Anderson.

"And we will, Captain. Major Hazard will continue the interrogation tomorrow. As for you, the matter is out of your hands. You will leave in the morning with the rest of us. General Lee has requested an early church service. I've talked to the minister and he's agreed to perform a private ceremony for the general at six o'clock. Afterwards we'll head back to headquarters and rejoin the army."

Taylor dismissed them and returned to the map room to see how Lee was getting along. He found him in the adjoining room sitting comfortably in a rocking chair by the fireplace, where a small wood fire was slowly disintegrating. A Bible open across his lap, Lee peered over the rim of his spectacles as Taylor stepped into the room.

"I beg your pardon, General."

"Yes, Colonel?"

"Sir, I'd like to discuss with you the matter of this alleged spy at army headquarters."

Lee removed his spectacles and said, "Proceed, Colonel."

"Sir, the real question here is what to do about the

prisoner. Major Hazard's convinced the Yankee will eventually give us the name of the spy. But I have my doubts."

"The danger to me is over," Lee told him. "And I think you're right. The major will only be wasting his time."

"Hazard wants the prisoner tried for espionage and executed if he refuses to cooperate. After all, he *was* apprehended wearing the uniform of a Southern officer."

"I find the idea revolting, Colonel. I can't see what purpose it would serve at this stage of the war."

"Agreed, sir. In fact, I think I've a better idea in mind."

Lee listened with interest as Taylor explained his proposal.

"An interesting idea, Colonel," he said afterwards.

"Then you approve, sir?"

"I'll take it under consideration. But we'll talk more about it in the morning."

"Yes, sir." Taylor clicked his heels. "Sleep well, General."

"Just one more thing before you leave, Colonel."

"Of course, sir?"

"The prisoner, I don't recall you mentioning his name."

"His name is Westmoreland, Captain Jonathan Westmoreland. I'm told he hails from Pennsylvania."

"Westmoreland, eh?" Lee pursed his lips. "For some reason that name sounds familiar."

"Major Gibson said that Westmoreland had met you at West Point several years ago."

"Of course, now I remember." Lee managed a smile. "What a small world it can be at times, eh, Colonel?"

* * *

Following their meeting with Lee and Taylor, Hazard and Anderson journeyed to the hospital and were told by the orderly on duty that Westmoreland was asleep in his room. Hazard had the surgeon sent for and asked the man for an update on the prisoner's condition.

"He stopped vomiting an hour ago and seems to be much better," replied the doctor. "I reckon he'll be fit enough to be discharged in the morning."

Hazard thanked him, and then he and Anderson left the hospital. Outside, Hazard said good night to his friend and promptly excused himself, a good night's sleep on his mind. Anderson headed back to his quarters.

The evening air was damp: a hint that more rain was forthcoming. Anderson paused at the door of the building and glanced over his shoulder nervously, as if sensing trouble nearby. He took a deep breath to calm down, somehow opened the door with his fingers and walked inside.

To his surprise, he found his orderly, Jake Woodley, sitting comfortably at the writing desk, smoking a hand-rolled cigar. Woodley jumped off the stool at the sight of his boss and brought his boots together.

"Beg pardon, Cap'n."

"Never mind, Jake, it's all right."

Anderson plopped down on the bed with a grunt and sighed heavily. Woodley thought he was worried about something.

"I reckon you wanna be left alone, sir."

"Yes, you can leave, Corporal."

Cap in one hand, cigar in the other, Woodley turned and

started for the door. When he was there, he glanced back.

"Ain't there nothin' you don't need before I go, Cap'n? Some coffee...or maybe a bite to eat?"

"No, Jake, I'm fine. We've got a long ride tomorrow. I want you to get as much rest as you can before we leave in the morning."

"What about you, sir? I respectfully suggest—"

"No, I'm fine, Corporal. I'm just not tired right now. I might even go for a walk later."

"A fine night for it." Woodley grinned. "Good night, Cap'n."

When he was gone, Anderson took a few minutes to reorganize his thoughts. After a while he got off the bed, walked over to the window and peered out.

Dusk had settled over Willistown, making it difficult for him to see, but he could still make out the church steeple standing above the wall of maple trees across the road. It reminded him of what Taylor had said earlier. "General Lee has requested an early church service." Anderson smirked as the new idea took root in his head. Almost at once, he felt the lightning bolt rush through his body. He touched his chest to verify the pounding inside and headed for the door.

Wayne Gibson was in a fitful mood. Following supper, of which he had eaten little, he inspected the officers' corral to make sure his horse had been properly cared for by the groom on duty. Afterwards he took a walking tour of Willistown with his orderly, Corporal Ben Hodge.

To his chagrin, he found the town much too lightly

defended. Considering the important person who was staying there, it didn't sit well with him. From what he saw, Willistown had no strategic military value. It was but a pebble in the road, used specifically as a medical facility for the army's wounded and dying.

He thought about Westmoreland again, in particular his mission to assassinate Lee. Yes, if it hadn't been for the ambush, he and his team might have succeeded. But that was irrelevant now, water under the bridge.

He dismissed Hodge and returned to his quarters, still not tired enough to sleep. After a while he stepped outside and sat under a leafless red maple, enjoying the crisp night air. He heard banjo music playing, a slow, sad tune that was unfamiliar to him. Somewhere beyond the music a lone dog sang a different kind of melody.

He saw someone approaching the hospital. It was a lanky silhouette of a man, barely obvious in the rapidly fading dusk. The silhouette, showing no hand at the bottom of his left sleeve, paused at the door of the building, where he was confronted by the sentry. Gibson watched with interest as the sentry saluted and opened the door, letting the invalid inside. He lit a cigar.

I wonder what he's up to.

"Fetch the surgeon, Private."

The medical orderly withdrew and returned moments later with the head surgeon.

"Yes, Captain, what is it?" queried the doctor.

"I need to see the prisoner," Anderson told him.

"Sorry, sir, but I can't allow it. Captain Westmoreland needs his rest. You can see him in the morning."

"No, I can't wait that long, it's too important." The red-faced surgeon started to protest, but Anderson cut him off before he could finish. "Don't worry, doctor, I'll take full responsibility."

The surgeon, a lieutenant of rank, seemed reluctant to comply, but then changed his mind, knowing it would not benefit him to argue with a senior officer. When he was gone, Anderson headed for the prisoner's room.

He was met at the door by the guard on duty. Anderson explained his reason for being there and waited for the soldier to open the door. Inside, the guard struck a match and lit the oil lamp that hung from the ceiling, bringing life to the room and rousing Westmoreland. Anderson dismissed the guard, who left promptly, closing the door after him. Westmoreland sat up in the bed, squinting at the one-armed man.

"What is it?" he implored.

"Sorry to disturb you, Captain, but I need to speak with you."

"I've already told you everything I know, sir. I've nothing more to say."

"I'm not here to interrogate you," said Anderson. "I just thought we might get better acquainted."

Westmoreland waited as Anderson sat down on the empty stool beside the bed. The rebel cleared his throat.

"Major Hazard and I had an audience with General Lee earlier," he said. "We discussed the war, among other things. For the South it does not go well."

"What makes you think I care?"

"Because you're a man of intelligence, Captain. I'm giving you the facts of life in the Confederate army. The average soldier is starving and wears rags for clothes. Supply trains out of Petersburg carry less food and munitions each day the war drags on, hardly enough to meet the army's requirements."

"So?"

"I'm offering you valuable information, Captain. Don't you find it interesting?"

"You're forgetting, sir, I'm a prisoner of the Confederate States of America, my enemy. The war is over for me. The information is meaningless."

"True, but what if you escaped and were able to make it back to Union headquarters? I'm sure the information would be of great value to General Grant."

Westmoreland corkscrewed his head, frowning.

"Exactly what are you trying to say, Captain? Why did you bother to come here?"

Anderson seemed not to have heard him.

He said, "I'm leaving with General Lee's entourage in the morning to resume my duties at army headquarters. However, Major Hazard will remain behind to continue the interrogation process."

"Oh?"

Anderson went on, "The major is still of the opinion that if you don't cooperate, you should be tried for espionage and hanged. Tell me, Captain, how do you feel about that?"

"I don't think you care how I feel. Besides, do you honestly believe I'd get a fair trial?" Anderson said nothing in return, and Westmoreland continued, "You've still not answered my question, sir. Why did you come here?"

"Why, it's simple. I've come to offer you an alternative."

"What are you talking about?"

Anderson dragged the stool closer to the bed, was now within arm's length of the prisoner. He reached inside his coat pocket and produced the derringer, holding it clumsily with his fingers. Westmoreland's jaw collapsed.

"Good God!" he spouted.

"Keep your voice down!" scolded Anderson. He handed over the derringer, butt first. "Be careful—it's loaded."

Westmoreland stared at the derringer, examining both barrels.

"Is this your alternative, Captain Anderson? Do you expect me to commit suicide with this to save myself from the hangman?"

"It's one option you have, surely. However, you don't seem like the kind of man who would do it. No, I'm thinking you could use the gun to help you escape, commandeer a horse, with which I would provide you, and return to General Grant with the information I've given you."

"You're joking, of course?"

"No, it's no joke, I assure you. In fact, when Major Stairs learns of your escape, he'll no doubt recommend that you receive another medal of honor."

"How do you know Major Stairs?"

"Actually, I've never met him, and he's never met me. In fact, he doesn't even know my real name."

Pin-drop quiet.

During the interlude they exchanged stares, with Westmoreland's still showing incredulity. It was then it occurred to him what Anderson was all about.

"*You* are the spy, Captain Anderson? *You* are the one Major Stairs calls Angel?"

More silence.

On his feet again, Anderson stepped over to the door, leaned against it and listened. Moments later he was back on the stool.

Westmoreland heard him say, "There is, however, a third alternative. With that gun you could finish the job you were sent here to do—assassinate General Lee."

Westmoreland laughed.

"Now I *know* you're joking, sir. Tell me, exactly how do I go about it? Just walk through his wall of guards, say good day to the general and pull the trigger?"

"Actually, there's a simpler way, Captain." Anderson leaned closer and whispered, "At six o'clock tomorrow morning, Lee will attend service in the chapel. I'll arrange to have you inside before he gets there. What happens after that will be up to you."

"I see." Westmoreland paused to put his thoughts in order. At last he said, "What about you, Captain Anderson? Eventually your peers will put two and two together and come looking for you."

"Naturally."

"But if they find you, you'll hang for treason. No one ever cries over the grave of man who willingly betrayed his country."

"No, you have it all wrong, Captain, I'm a patriot, *not* a traitor. I did what I did because I detest this war and what it's done to me and countless others like me. But the price we paid is small compared to those who died for a cause that no longer has meaning. If Lee dies tomorrow, God willing, the war will end and thousands on both sides would be spared. Then the two nations will reunite, and you and I will become countrymen again."

Westmoreland was at a loss for words. Knowing he had gotten his point across, Anderson rose off the stool.

"Until tomorrow morning," he said, and left the room.

Westmoreland stared at the derringer but soon tired of it. He tucked the weapon inside his right sock, at the same time thinking about what he would do in the morning. He slipped off the bed, dropped to his knees and prayed.

XXIV

Bill Anderson's three alternatives kept Westmoreland awake for most of the night. By tomorrow dawn he would be faced with the most consequential decision of his life. Would he be able to muster up the courage and commit the ungodly act of suicide? Or would he use the derringer to help him make his escape and return to friendlier company? Or would he try to finish the job he had volunteered to do from the outset, assassinate Robert E. Lee?

He juggled the options again. His first alternative was not viable, one he promptly discarded. As Anderson had said, he was not the type who could end his life with one trigger pull.

On the other hand, his second option was more to his liking. With good luck and a fast horse, he could make it back to the Union lines with the information Anderson had provided him and live to see another day. Westmoreland felt the smile blossom on his lips as he pictured the scene of his lovely wife embracing him...

He lifted his trouser leg and removed the derringer from its hiding place as he contemplated his third option. To assassinate Lee, an idle thought ever since he had lost O'Grady and the others, was a distinct possibility again. Yet to complete the job, he would need to get close to the target, for the derringer was effective only at short range. Could he get close enough to shoot Lee? Anderson had said that he would arrange for him to be inside the chapel before Lee arrived, but could the one-armed man be trusted? Or, in fact, was there a fourth alternative?

Westmoreland pondered, the wheels in his mind churning at full speed. Yes, there was indeed a fourth option to consider. He could expose Anderson as the spy, thus saving himself from the hangman. The drawback was that they would chuck him in prison camp for the duration of the war. Only how long would that be? A few weeks? Several months? A long year? He had heard the gruesome tales of Union soldiers dying in Southern prison camps from disease, starvation and maltreatment. After all he had been through, would he have enough physical and mental strength to survive prison life?

Dear God, what am I to do?

* * *

Anderson awoke early on that fateful Sunday morning of 6 November. First things first, he summoned his orderly to help him with his uniform. The job completed, he instructed Woodley to have his horse saddled and ready by six o'clock.

"You goin' somewhere, Cap'n?"

"That's right, Corporal."

"But, sir, I'm goin' with you, ain't I?"

"No, not this time."

Woodley shrugged, knowing from experience not to challenge his superior. He finished clothing the spy with boots and coat, and then left to fulfill his first assignment of the new day.

Anderson retrieved his journal from its hiding place, opened it and sighed. Yes, the military information he had recorded was significant indeed, would be of great value upon his arrival in Union-held territory. No doubt it would determine how the Yankees would treat him. He shoved the journal inside his coat lining and headed for the door.

It was twenty minutes to six when he stepped inside the hospital. Not surprisingly, he noticed a different soldier standing guard outside the prisoner's room. Anderson started toward him, but stopped when he was intercepted by the head surgeon. Surprisingly, it was the same one he had traded words with the previous evening.

"Is there something you require, Captain?"

"The prisoner, is he awake, doctor?"

"Yes."

"Is he fit enough to leave?"

"Yes, quite fit. I examined him just five minutes ago."

"Very well, doctor. As of this moment, I'm taking him into my charge."

"Sorry, sir, but I can't allow it unless you sign for his release."

"I've no time for that!" barked Anderson. "You take care of the paperwork. I'll assume full responsibility for the prisoner."

The surgeon conferred with himself, wondering if he should obey the arrogant, one-armed man or continue to challenge him. He decided on the easy way out.

"As you wish, sir."

When he was gone, Anderson confronted the guard outside the prisoner's room and explained his reason for being there. The corporal nodded obediently and opened the door for him.

"Stay here," Anderson told him. "I'll need your help in a few minutes." He stepped inside the room and the guard closed the door behind him.

Westmoreland had been awake for several hours and was on his feet as the invalid approached. Anderson noted the Yankee's bloodshot eyes and the sagging bags under them, knowing what it meant.

"You have the gun, Captain?" he asked.

Westmoreland showed the bulge in his sock.

Satisfied, Anderson stepped over to the window and drew the curtains. The sleeping hamlet of Willistown was shrouded in darkness. There were several campfires aglow in the main bivouac area down the road, signs of the soldiery awakening to greet the new dawn. He closed the curtains, and as he walked away from the window, Westmoreland noted the anxious face, the right arm trembling at will. Even his words quivered when spoke.

"Let's get to the chapel, Captain. We've not much time before Lee will be there."

"What makes you think I want to kill him?"

"Because Lee is the devil. You *must* kill the devil! Major Gibson was right, you're an officer dedicated to his duty. To not go through with it would be an act of cowardice."

Westmoreland ignored him.

"And you, Captain, what about you?"

"I am a spy, sir, perhaps the most despicable human being on the face of God's earth. As you said last night, I will be branded a traitor by my countrymen. After I get you inside the chapel, I will make my escape and leave this place forever. I will never see my home or family again."

"But they'll hunt you down, sir, and when they find you, you know what they'll do to you."

"I'd rather take my chances, if you don't mind." Anderson paused to allow his breath to catch up with him. "Now, when we're inside the chapel, I'll distract the guard. At that moment you must be quick. Kill him if you have to. Understand?"

Westmoreland nodded.

"Good, let's go."

Outside the room, Anderson told the sentry that he was taking the prisoner to the interrogation hut and would he please accompany them. The corporal nodded without a word of protest, and Anderson led the way out. It was after they were outside the hospital and ten yards down the road when Anderson stopped, halting their momentum.

He said to the guard, "The prisoner will be tried today and no doubt sentenced to hang for his crime. He's asked me if I would take him to the chapel so he can beg God to forgive him. Since he's an officer, I've agreed to grant his request." He showed the guard a fake grin. "This won't take long, Corporal."

"Yes, sir."

At the front step of the chapel, Anderson asked the guard to open the door, which he did, and told them to "wait here." Inside, he found the rows of pews empty. No one was about, not even the minister. Obviously the cleric had bought his lie that Lee's private service would take place at seven o'clock rather than at six as previously arranged. There was a single candle alight on the altar, the rest of the place masked in shadows. The ideal place for an ambush.

He went back to the door, wiggled his fingers, and Westmoreland stepped through the portal, the guard a body's length behind him. The corporal shut the door after them, and Anderson made his play.

Clutching his abdomen, he doubled over in a show of pain, an excellent performance worthy of an actor, and the corporal reacted on instinct. A huge mistake.

Westmoreland, quick as a cat, rushed the guard at battering-ram speed and the inevitable followed. The guard went flying ten feet back from the impact and crashed to the floor, losing his rifle in the process. Without hesitation, Westmoreland took possession of the weapon and readied himself for the soldier's counterattack. The corporal, having regained his equilibrium, vaulted to his feet and charged his enemy, hands extended and ready to kill. He ended up back on the floor when Westmoreland smacked him flush in the face with the rifle butt, rendering him unconscious.

Anderson cried, "Hurry, Captain, Lee will be here any minute!"

Westmoreland grabbed hold of the corporal's boots, dragged him three rows forward and shoved him under the pew, out of sight. Next he retrieved the rifle—it had been damaged during the scuffle—and placed it alongside the lifeless soldier. He lifted his trouser leg and yanked out the derringer, oblivious of his trembling hands. When he got back on his feet, Anderson was not there.

He heard muted voices outside, chaperoned by the ominous sounds of approaching footsteps. He dashed up the center aisle, circled behind the altar and crouched into a fighting position, fading into the shadows. From there he could see anyone coming down the aisle without being spotted. The perfect place to spring the trap.

He glanced around him. To his right was a carved wooden door, a silver crucifix hanging from the wall above it. He presumed it led to the minister's private chambers. On his far left was a solitary window, the glass mirroring the candlelight on the altar, preventing him from seeing out. Westmoreland took a deep breath to calm his nerves and waited for General Lee.

Wayne Gibson had endured a restless sleep. Tired of tossing

back and forth, he climbed out of the bed and was dressed by half past five, prepared for a long day in the saddle. He donned his coat and cap and stepped outside.

Another cool morning. Bright stars hovered overhead in a clear black sky, and a thin strip of gray dawn was slowly maturing on the horizon. Gibson spotted the twinkling light in the chapel window and deduced that the minister was preparing for first service. He thought about attending, but quickly decided against it. He needed to get an early start, was itching to get back with his regiment. He headed for the officers' mess.

Inside, he found the cook working, a pair of orderlies assisting. In the corner furthest from him was Robert Hazard. The interrogator was sitting alone, a plate of scrambled eggs and cornbread in front of him. He was one of only two officers in attendance. Gibson started toward him.

"Good morning, Major Hazard. May I join you?"

Hazard swallowed the food in his mouth and said, "Please do." Gibson sat down. A mess orderly soon appeared and asked him if he wanted breakfast.

"No, just coffee," Gibson told him.

The man withdrew and returned moments later with a tin cup of hot coffee. Gibson thanked him before he left and carefully sampled the dark brew.

Hazard said, "I see you're an early riser too."

"Didn't sleep well," said Gibson. "Got a lot on my mind."

Hazard filled his mouth with a slice of cornbread and washed it down with a swig of coffee. He wiped his mouth with a napkin.

Gibson heard him say, "Are you planning to leave today?"

"I was under the impression I had no choice."

Hazard said nothing in return, was involved with another mouthful of breakfast. Gibson changed the subject.

"About Captain Westmoreland, sir."

"Yes, Major?"

"I was wondering. Are you and Captain Anderson planning to interrogate him today?"

"It is my intention to do so," Hazard told him. "However, the captain is leaving this morning with General Lee and his party. They're due back at army headquarters."

"So that explains why he was at the hospital last night."

"Oh?" Hazard frowned. "What do you mean?"

"I happened to be outside last night and saw him going into the hospital. It was late dusk, I recall. I assumed he went there to interrogate Westmoreland."

"I was not aware of that."

"Really." Gibson hesitated, but then said, "You know, Major, there's something troubling me about this whole spy business."

"Yes?"

"Well, I still can't understand why the Yankees dispatched a detail of sharpshooters to assassinate General Lee. Why didn't they just let the spy do it instead?"

"I reckon because it would've compromised his cover."

"Still, wouldn't it be easier for one man to do the job?" Gibson shook his head, then answered his own question. "No, if it were up to me, I'd let the spy try his luck. I wouldn't risk the lives of six men."

Hazard's face clouded.

"Exactly what are you trying to say, Major Gibson?"

"Well, I did a lot of thinking last night and came to the conclusion that maybe the spy can't kill Lee because he's incapable of doing it."

"I don't follow."

"Well, say the spy was an invalid, like Anderson for instance. In my mind, that would be the reason why Grant dispatched Westmoreland and his team to do the job."

"Indeed!" Hazard adjusted his spectacles. "Are you suggesting that Bill Anderson is the spy?"

"I'm suggesting nothing, sir. But if there's an enemy agent at army headquarters, how can you be sure it's *not* Anderson? He has the ideal job, knows the latest intelligence. You just said you were unaware he was at the hospital last night. Don't you find that worth investigating?"

"So what you're really saying is that Anderson might have gone to the hospital not to interrogate the prisoner, but to provide him with some sort of weapon to kill Lee with." Hazard laughed at his own words. "No, I can't believe that."

"Perhaps, but are you willing to bet the general's life on it?" Gibson leaned closer. "Tell me, Major, do you know where Anderson is now? Do you know where Lee is?"

Hazard opened his mouth to answer, but never got the words out when the visitor appeared in the mess tent.

He was an elderly, white-haired gentleman. He wore black clothes, matching shoes, and a white collar wrapped snugly around the bottom half of his neck. To the majors, it was obvious who he was and what he represented, but it was

Hazard who seemed more interested in the man's sudden appearance.

He said, "Can I help you with something, reverend?"

"I'm looking for Colonel Taylor," answered the minister. "Do you know where I might find him?"

"He should be with General Lee." Hazard stared at the holy man, a wrinkled brow fastened to his pallid face. "I don't understand, reverend. Are you not having a private service for the general this morning?"

"Yes, but the time was changed to seven o'clock."

Hazard, still confused, glanced at an equally bemused Gibson, who said, "By whom, reverend?"

"I don't remember his name, but he was an officer."

"Who?" implored Hazard.

"Why, the man with one arm."

"Oh, my God!" The shouted words were Gibson's. He vaulted to his feet. "Find Anderson!" he told Hazard. "If my guess is correct, he'll be making his escape."

"But...I don't understand," said the preacher. "Is there something wrong?"

There was no time for small talk. Gibson shoved him aside, undid his holster flap and yanked out his Colt revolver. Hazard jumped out of his chair.

"Where are you going, Major?"

But there was no answer, couldn't be, for Gibson had already turned away and was sprinting for the exit.

XXV

Robert E. Lee awakened early on Sunday feeling much better than the previous day. After dressing himself, he went outside to grab some fresh air. Upon his return, he found Taylor waiting for him in the map room. Also there were three junior staff officers and his personal bodyguard. Following a brief conference to discuss the day's itinerary, Lee gave the order and they left the building together. It was a few minutes before six o'clock when they arrived at their destination.

Lee was the first to enter the chapel, followed in step by the faithful Taylor. The others remained outside, as ordered.

Lee scanned the rows of empty pews, surprised by the quietness of the place.

"No one seems to be about," he said unnecessarily. "Are we too early, Colonel?"

Taylor produced a pocket watch, opened it and noted the time.

"No, sir, we're right on time."

"Strange."

"General, shall I have the minister sent for? If you wish, I'll fetch him myself."

"No, Colonel, that won't be necessary. Please tell the others to get some breakfast. I don't want our timetable disrupted because of this. Allow me five minutes to say a few prayers in private."

"Of course, sir." Taylor stepped outside and relayed Lee's order to the others. They left promptly, and he went back inside and closed the door. "Take as long as you need, General. I'll wait for you here."

Lee removed his hat and started up the center aisle. From his spot behind the altar, Westmoreland saw the target approaching. Despite the drab light, he recognized the man's silver and white hair and beard, the jutted chin, the classic military demeanor. Incredible! The moment he had prepared for was finally at hand. He wiped the sweat from his brow and sighed nervously. His mouth was a desert, the derringer unsteady in his trembling hand.

Lee stopped suddenly, thinking he had heard something, but then decided he had not and resumed the journey. Westmoreland watched each regimented step, unaware that he, too, was being observed from the side window.

Gibson, having arrived at the chapel just seconds earlier, had the perfect view of the scene unfolding before him. He checked to make sure his Colt was loaded and cocked the hammer, his heart and brain running at locomotive speed.

Lee stopped when he reached the front-row pews. He chose the one on his left and slowly squeezed in. Westmoreland and Gibson watched as the supreme commander of the Confederate army fell to his knees with clasped hands and bowed in prayer.

Westmoreland rose out of his crouch without a sound. Gibson felt the perspiration pouring from his skin when he recognized his rival's pale face in the candlelight. Taylor, still standing at the rear of the chapel, also saw the Yankee cavalryman. Instinctively, he rushed forward at the double quick, was nearly halfway up the aisle when Westmoreland showed him the derringer, halting his momentum.

"That's far enough, Colonel!"

The complementary echo that followed bounced against the walls of the holy chamber, interrupting Lee's private chat with God. Amazingly, the rebel leader showed no sign of fear at the sight of Westmoreland and his deadly handgun. Perhaps more amazing was the calm tone in his voice when he spoke.

"Captain Westmoreland, I presume?"

"Yes, sir." Westmoreland inclined his head in deference to the great man and his rank.

Taylor hollered, "You won't get away with it, Captain! It won't solve anything! I implore you to surrender!"

"Stay where you are!" Westmoreland shouted back.

"I admire your courage," Lee told him. "Most of all, I admire your dedication to your duty."

"I regret what I must do, General. Please believe me, sir."

"Allow me the dignity to stand up and face you properly."

Westmoreland nodded his consent and waited as Lee climbed to his feet. At that moment barely five yards separated them.

"No!" cried Taylor, and it was then Gibson made his move.

He crashed through the window like a runaway steer and landed headfirst on his hands and knees, the Colt spinning from his grasp. Lee did not hesitate and rushed out of the pew, heading toward Gibson in an obvious attempt to help him. His gun hand still shaking, Westmoreland fired the derringer but missed the target by six inches, the bullet lodging in a pew of solid oak eight rows back.

Taylor was fumbling with his holster flap as he dashed up the aisle, aware that Westmoreland was cocking the derringer, preparing for another, his final shot. Back on his feet, Gibson lunged toward Lee, entering the line of fire as Westmoreland squeezed the trigger.

The bullet exploded in the meat of his chest cavity, splintering the rib nearest to his heart. Westmoreland and Lee watched in horror as Gibson fell back against the pew from the impact and slumped to the floor. Just then Taylor appeared on the scene, revolver in hand. Westmoreland gave him the derringer, butt first, and then crouched beside the man he had wounded, tears welling in his eyes.

"I'm sorry, Wayne."

"I...knew you would do it, Jon." Gibson's words were barely audible. He coughed blood as he struggled to catch his breath. "Like I said before, we're two of a kind."

Suddenly, there were soldiers everywhere. Taylor barked out a series of commands, Westmoreland was manhandled and taken away, and Lee was escorted to a place of safety. Taylor then sent a runner to the hospital to fetch the surgeon, who arrived three minutes later with medical bag in hand. After examining Gibson's wound, he rose off the floor and confronted Lee's adjutant. The mood on his face was grim.

"Well?" urged Taylor.

"The major's wound is mortal," said the surgeon. "There's nothing I can do for him."

Incredibly, Gibson's lips moved, and Taylor heard him say, "Is General Lee all right?"

"Yes, Major, the general is unharmed."

"I'm glad."

Gibson smiled, a faint, gallant smile, took his last breath and closed his eyes.

It was late in the afternoon when Robert Hazard walked into the prisoner's hut. He confronted the guard at the door and told him to leave and wait outside. When the soldier was gone, the interrogator stepped around the desk and calmly removed his cap. Westmoreland, sitting in the chair opposite, waited as the rebel sat down and donned his spectacles.

"General Lee and his party have finally left Willistown," he said. "Regrettably, it was much later than planned."

Westmoreland was uninterested.

"What about Gibson?" he urged.

"I'm afraid the major didn't make it," was Hazard's reply. A brief pause before he continued, "You know, Captain, you were almost successful today. Thanks to Major Gibson, General Lee is a lucky man."

"And Anderson?"

"Well, it seems that he somehow managed to slip across the Federal lines despite our efforts to fetch him back."

"Too bad."

"Yes. However, not all was lost. In his haste to make his escape, he left behind him a rather detailed journal of his espionage activities the past five months. It was found in the road."

"But you didn't realize he was the spy until today. He had you fooled right up to the last moment."

"True. Oddly enough, it was Gibson who suspected him of being the spy, though I admit I was skeptical at the time."

"What about me, Major? What are you going to do with me?"

"Well, there are some of us who feel you should be tried and executed for what you did today. However, since General Lee survived, we've decided it's not necessary."

"Prison camp?"

"No." Hazard adjusted his spectacles. "By order of Colonel Taylor, I'm to arrange a deal with the enemy for your release in exchange for two Southern officers."

"A prisoner exchange?" Westmoreland chuckled. "You're joking?"

"No, Captain, it's no joke. Tomorrow morning a

messenger will be dispatched to the Union lines. On his person will be a letter addressed to Ulysses S. Grant. It will explain in full detail the terms of the exchange."

"Colonel Taylor was most generous."

"Actually, from what he told me, it was General Lee's idea."

"Oh?"

"Yes." Hazard pursed his lips. "Personally speaking, I find that ironic, considering what almost happened to him today."

Westmoreland scratched his head, but not because he had an itch.

He said, "For whom will I be exchanged, Major?"

"Well, one of them is an artillery officer who just happens to be a relative of President Davis."

"And the other man?"

Hazard seemed hesitant to reply, but then took a deep breath and said when he exhaled, "Captain Anderson."

"Oh?" Westmoreland thought. Finally he said, "What makes you think that General Grant will agree to your terms?"

"Oh, he will, rest assured," said the poker-faced Hazard. "Let's face it, he's getting a good bargain in return. A loyal, competent officer in exchange for two of ours, of whom one was once a good friend of mine. Unfortunately for him, Bill Anderson will always be remembered as a traitor to his country."

"You could be wrong about all this, sir."

"No, I don't think so. You see, Joshua Stairs will insist that Grant agrees to the terms of the exchange. He has the general's complete confidence, I understand."

"How do you know about Major Stairs?"

"Why, from Captain Anderson, of course."

"I don't understand."

"Well, it seems that Anderson included his name several times in his diary. His scribbling, I'm told, was most difficult to decipher. Needless to say, it will be the incriminating evidence that sends him to the gallows."

"What about you, Major?"

"My job is finished here, Captain, we were able to root out the spy. Mind you, we were lucky. In the morning I'm returning to General Longstreet's command to resume my regular duties."

"To serve a lost cause?" Westmoreland grunted. "Don't you find *that* ironic, sir?"

"Perhaps, but I've known the war was lost for quite some time now. You see, I was at Gettysburg too."

"Then why continue the fight? Eventually Grant will destroy Lee's army, with many lives on both sides lost in the process. You're an intelligent man, Major, doesn't that bother you?"

"Indeed it does. I've lost two brothers in this war who fought for a cause they believed in. But as Gibson once said, the south will rise from the ashes of this war. It's General Lee who will decide when she has suffered enough."

Westmoreland made no comment in return, just watched as Hazard removed his spectacles and wiped away the tear as it fell from his eye.

Peter Wilson was the first of the picket soldiers to see the white flag flapping in the distance. About a quarter mile away, he estimated. In all, the approaching party consisted of three gray-clad soldiers and one in Union blue. Wilson confronted the lone officer at the campfire.

"They're coming, Major."

The man whom Wilson had addressed stood out of his crouch and joined the sergeant at the side of the road. Wilson indicated the flag of truce.

"Yes, I see them," said Joshua Stairs.

He removed the cigar from his mouth, tossed it away and

turned up the collar of his greatcoat, shielding his neck from the icy wind.

Wilson said, "Sir, is that your man with 'em?"

"Hard to say at this range." Stairs stared through his field glasses and saw what he had hoped to see. "Yes, it's him! I see him now!" Smiling, he said to Wilson, "All right, Sergeant, bring the prisoners forward."

Wilson left and promptly returned with them.

Stairs looked them over. The tall, round-faced colonel, the man reputed to be a relative of Jefferson Davis, was of little interest to him. His concern was for the stone-faced, one-armed captain. Bill Anderson was ghostly pale, had the unhealthy look of death about him, unlike the colonel who seemed indifferent to the proceedings. Hatless, Anderson stood ramrod straight, his dark hair billowing in the wind like a tattered battle flag. Stairs indicated the four men approaching along the snow-covered road.

"There, gentlemen."

Anderson said, "You don't have to go through with this, Major."

"'Fraid it's out of my hands, Captain. Orders are orders."

The party of four was less than twenty yards away. Stairs observed the young soldier toting the flag, battling to hold it steady against the angry wind. He looked no older than his kid sister. Behind the flag bearer was another young soldier, an officer, followed in step by Jon Westmoreland and another Johnny Reb. As much as he could tell, none of the enemy soldiers was toting a firearm. He felt the smile growing on his lips at the sight of his friend approaching.

The wind gusted, forcing him to grab hold of his cap. He shot a glance at Anderson, amazed at the man's calm exterior. A brave man, no doubt, only what was he feeling inside? Guilt? Remorse for his crime? Hate for the cause he had once served? Or was it hate for General Grant, who had agreed to the terms of the exchange? Stairs sighed, knowing that much which had taken place was his doing. But that was war, and he was only doing his duty.

The rebel officer in charge of the party ordered a halt five yards from the Yankee pickets. He glanced from side to side, remembering it was not that long ago when he had been dispatched on another mission of truce. He walked up to Stairs, and they exchanged salutes. The rebel took a short moment to clear the frog from his throat, and then he spoke, only the wind snatched the words from his mouth. Stairs leaned closer.

"What was that, Lieutenant?"

"My name is Crenshaw, sir."

"Mine is Stairs."

"Major, it would be a favor to my sore throat if we could get this over with as soon as possible."

"Agreed."

Crenshaw glanced over his shoulder and beckoned his prisoner to join them. Five steps later Westmoreland was standing within arm's length of the Confederate officers, his eyes focused on Anderson. The former spy spoke first.

"So, Captain, we meet again."

"Yes, sir."

Anderson went on, "As you remember, I was compelled

to leave Willistown in a hurry. Before they take me away, I'd be obliged if you'd satisfy my curiosity. Were you successful?"

"No, fate had other plans."

"Explain."

"I had two chances to kill him. The first time my aim was off. When I fired again, Gibson was in the way."

"Gibson, huh?" Anderson pursed his lips. "Strange, but I never trusted him. It was as if he knew all long who I was."

"Sir, you realize what's going to happen when you cross the picket line?"

"Of course, the fortunes of war. I was, you might say, the Cassius of this play, and you, Captain, were my dagger. But unlike Shakespeare's villain of fate, I was not successful. It just wasn't meant to be."

No more words were needed. Westmoreland stepped aside and watched as Anderson lumbered past him, the stoic-faced colonel following in his wake.

Stairs said to Crenshaw, "Our business is concluded."

"Yes, sir."

Crenshaw saluted, waited for Stairs to return the gesture, which he did, and then he turned and marched away, retracing his footsteps for the others of his party to follow. Stairs confronted Wilson.

"Sergeant, give Captain Westmoreland a cup of coffee." He smiled at his friend, and they shook hands. "Welcome home, Jon."

Ulysses S. Grant lifted the tumbler to his mouth and drank. He coughed when the whiskey exploded in his stomach, then gave his attention to the pair of young officers facing him across the desk. He reached for the whiskey bottle.

"Would you care for a dram, gentlemen?"

"None for me," Stairs told him.

"What about you, Captain?"

"Yes, sir, a small one, please."

Grant filled another tumbler and gave it to him. Smiling, Westmoreland raised the glass to his lips and tossed the whiskey in his mouth.

"Thank you, sir."

"You've been through a lot, surely," said Grant, speaking to his empty glass. "The army is in your debt."

"But I didn't succeed, General. Worse, I lost five good men. I'm not proud of that."

"It could have happened to anyone, Jon," said Stairs, butting in. "It wasn't your fault, and you know it. You did your duty."

"The major is right," said Grant. "You're not to blame for what happened. It is I who must bear the responsibility."

"With all due respect, sir, your words don't ease the pain," Jon told him. "I'll live with the memory for the rest of my life."

"I know, son."

Stairs said, "Not all was lost, General. Anderson *did* supply us with some valuable information. For instance, the state of the Reb army at Petersburg."

"Yes, but most of it was what we had surmised beforehand, Major. It won't shorten the war. Although Lee's army is starving, the enemy will continue the fight until he determines otherwise. The question is when."

The great man fixed himself another whiskey. He raised the tumbler but stopped short of his lips, as if forgetting something. He swung his eyes to Westmoreland.

He said, "I served with General Lee in Mexico many years ago, but I must admit I don't remember much about him. Tell me, Captain, what was your impression?"

"I really can't say, General, my time with him was brief. However, Major Gibson, the man who died in his place, did so willingly—he didn't hesitate. And that, sir, tells me everything I need to know about General Lee."

"Indeed, but I think you're right, Captain." Grant emptied his tumbler. "You're absolutely right."

The railway platform was crowded with human beings, the impatient ones using their pointed elbows like bayonets to get closer to the tracks as the passenger train braked into the station.

Alice Westmoreland did not bother to fight through the mob. She just stood where she had been standing for the last three hours, hoping to catch a glimpse of her husband. Would he be on the train? His letter of two weeks ago had told her he would be arriving in Harrisburg this day. Then again, she was an army wife and knew peculiar things happened in the military.

The soldiers began to disembark, one by one. Alice watched with envy as spouses and loved ones found each other and embraced. Then came the kissing, the laughter, the crying. Many of the soldiers had come back from the war wrapped in bandages, some with limps attached, others with limbs missing. She wondered what she would see when her husband appeared.

Dear God, please let him be well!

The crowd began to disperse. She had just about given up hope when she saw him standing at the other end of the platform, gear in one hand, waving at her with the other. She started toward him slowly, then faster with each step, his handsome face becoming obscured as the tears got in the way.

"Oh, Jonathan!"

Westmoreland dropped his gear, and she rushed into his waiting arms. Tears cascaded from their eyes.

"Are you here to stay, my love?" Her voice was anxious.

"Yes, Alice, for me the war is over." He kissed her on the forehead with affection. "Let's go home."

"We form one country now. Abandon all these local animosities, and make your sons Americans."

Robert E. Lee

THE LOGO

The defining theme of the T. K. MARION logo is education. The cowboy sitting astride a horse galloping across an open book is a metaphor depicting the author as a relentless crusader advocating the universal principle that knowledge based on the teachings of history is a never-ending process, and that the power it wields is unbounded [and] must be employed solely for the betterment of the human race.

The halo of stars along the brim of the logo represents the Thirteen Stars Scholarship Foundation, a nonprofit entity pioneered by the author, of which he is president and CEO. Scholarships awarded by the foundation will benefit persons with cystic fibrosis, a disease which deprived his brother, James, of a longer life. Partial proceeds from *KILL THE DEVIL* and subsequent novels authored by T. K. Marion will subsidize the foundation.

T. K. Marion's next novel
EAST WIND, RAIN
is a Cold War espionage thriller.